"I can't remember when I didn't want you, Serena."

The wind caught a few strands of her hair, and David brushed them back, resting his hand on her cheek. "And if you think I'm relaxed, well..."

He glanced downward, and she followed his gaze. *Hello.* Even the thickness of the denim couldn't hide the erection straining against his zipper.

It was in a desire-blurred haze that Serena registered him laying her back on the soft blanket, pressing his weight against her. He surprised her by taking her hand and placing it against her breast, which ached for attention, the pebbled peak thrusting forward.

"Other women don't affect me like this. Just you. And I don't believe other men make you feel this way."

Definitely not. Serena stared into his eyes, but couldn't bring herself to admit the truth.

"Do you get this aroused with anyone else, Serena? This hot?"

It was a guess on his part, but an accurate one. She *was* hot and she was ready for more....

Dear Reader,

My author motto is Passion, Laughter and Happily Ever After.
I work to include these elements in all of my books, but no
couple I've written about before has shared a passion quite
as intense as Serena Donavan and David Grant's.

Friends since college, Serena and David had a very hot
one-night stand the last time he visited her in Georgia, and
though neither of them can forget the intimate encounter,
Serena insists it was a mistake. She's free spirited and
easygoing in many ways, but her past has left her guarded
about serious relationships—especially with someone like
David, whose affluent corporate lifestyle is very different from
her own. Now, with his company relocating to Atlanta, David
has the perfect chance to reignite the sparks between him
and Serena. When he hires her to help organize a charity
auction his company is sponsoring, his ulterior motive is
to seduce her into taking a chance on love. And seduce
her he does.

I hope you'll visit my Web site at www.tanyamichaels.com
to read more about how your purchase of this book helps
raise money to fight breast cancer, like the bachelor auction
my heroine and hero plan, and I hope you enjoy watching
Serena and David find their way to happily ever after.

Best wishes,

Tanya Michaels

Books by Tanya Michaels

HARLEQUIN TEMPTATION
968—HERS FOR THE WEEKEND
986—SHEER DECADENCE

TANYA MICHAELS

GOING ALL THE WAY

HARLEQUIN®

TORONTO • NEW YORK • LONDON
AMSTERDAM • PARIS • SYDNEY • HAMBURG
STOCKHOLM • ATHENS • TOKYO • MILAN • MADRID
PRAGUE • WARSAW • BUDAPEST • AUCKLAND

Like my fictional heroine, I greatly appreciate those artists—painters,
musicians, screenwriters, etc.—whose creative work can inspire us all.
But the most poignant inspiration comes from knowing so-called
ordinary people who cope with extraordinary trials. This book is in
loving memory of two women who faced devastating illness with
remarkable flashes of humor and unfathomable courage.

ISBN 0-373-69208-0

GOING ALL THE WAY

Copyright © 2005 by Tanya Michna.

This edition published by arrangement with Harlequin Books S.A.

® and TM are trademarks of the publisher. Trademarks indicated with
® are registered in the United States Patent and Trademark Office, the
Canadian Trade Marks Office and in other countries.

www.eHarlequin.com

Printed in U.S.A.

1

DAVID GRANT didn't believe in signs—unless of course they happened to suit his purpose, as was the case this April morning. The fact that his employers had voted to transfer their corporate headquarters to Atlanta of all places was definitely a good omen.

"Congratulations, David." Lou Innes, the *I* in AGI VoiceTech, polished his glasses with a linen handkerchief as he beamed at David from the opposite end of the conference table. The announcement that David would move from Boston to Georgia and spearhead the relocation also came with an almost guaranteed earlier-than-anticipated vice-presidential promotion. "I'm sure you're already working on exciting plans for our new location."

"Yes, sir." David flashed the confident grin he'd inherited from a long line of Grants. "I certainly am."

Atlanta offered unparalleled opportunity. Especially for David's love life.

When he'd gone to his parents' anniversary bash in Savannah last summer, he'd scheduled an extra day to spend with his best friend in Atlanta, as he'd been doing ever since he and Serena Donavan had attended Georgia Tech together. Normally on these layovers, Serena subjected him to whatever little hole-in-the-wall restaurant she was currently enamored with, and they caught up on any happenings they hadn't covered by e-mail. The next day, he would catch a cab to Hartsfield and fly back to Boston. His August visit had followed the familiar pattern.

Except, after the hole-in-the-wall restaurant and before the cab to the airport, they'd spent one incredible stormy night making love in Serena's studio loft apartment. That was new. According to the tense un-Serena-like e-mail that had awaited him when he got home, it had also been a mistake.

David disagreed. But with her stubborn streak, he'd need patience and finesse to bring her around to his way of thinking. Luckily, he had both.

Their first few exchanges following his trip had been awkward, and he sensed she would have avoided talking to him if he hadn't initiated contact. But as their friendship slowly resumed its former flirtatious tone, he'd been confident that, while he could have made faster progress in person, time was on his side. Then, right before he was scheduled to be in Georgia for Thanksgiving, she'd surprised him by announcing she'd started seeing someone.

As an overachiever who thought nothing of clocking sixty-hour weeks, David was used to his hard work paying off—this morning was a perfect example of the success he usually enjoyed.

With the meeting adjourned, the executives around the rectangular table began to disband, and the president of finance, Richard Gunn, approached, a wide grin beneath his graying moustache. "Congratulations. I don't have to tell you how rare it is that we give opportunities like this to someone as comparatively new to the company, but there's no question you're the man for the job."

"Thanks." David stood to shake the older man's hand. At thirty-three, David wasn't exactly fresh from college, but he knew he was younger than the other candidates they'd considered for the relocation. "I'll give it my all."

"We'd expect nothing less of you."

He'd never given them reason to—he'd been proving himself ever since his grad-school interview with the communications technology partnership of Andrews, Gunn and Innes. David had been eager to be a part of the strides the company was making in the field of voice-related software, and he'd been pleased by the fact that the firm was in Massachusetts. David had deliberately looked outside the southeast to make his mark, which made him something of an exception in his family.

The Grants of Savannah often had things handed to them by virtue of their social status and wealth, but he enjoyed the challenge of relying on his merits rather than on his name. A definite contrast to his older brother, Ben, who had made it clear that when he ran for Congress next year, he planned to milk his connection to the two previous Senators Grant for all it was worth. But David looked forward to returning to Georgia now and demonstrating just how successful he could be on his own.

"Do you have plans for lunch?" Richard asked. "In light of your possible promotion, I might even consider picking up the tab. Unless you'd rather celebrate with the lovely Tiffany? *I'd* ditch me for her any day of the week."

"Actually, Tiff and I, um, decided to part ways over the weekend." Tiffany had decided, anyway. David had been rather bemused when she broke up with him…mostly because he hadn't realized they were dating.

Richard frowned at his gaffe. "Oh. I'm sorry."

"No, it's for the best. I'm about to move, and Tiffany will find someone more suited to her in no time."

Tiffany Jode was intelligent, gorgeous and the heiress to a small fortune—small as compared to national budgets. She and David ran in the same social circles and had ended up in bed on several enjoyable occasions. But the evenings they'd spent together had as often been a product of coincidence as of deliberate planning, and he'd never thought of Tiffany and himself as a couple. So he certainly hadn't seen the breakup coming. He'd mentioned a few weeks ago that the AGI partners were considering Atlanta for their new headquarters, and that he'd enjoy returning to Georgia, if given the chance. On Saturday, when the subject had come up over their lunch at Turner Fisheries, she'd grown silent, barely touching the nearly famous clam chowder. On the way back to her place she asked if he'd even once considered inviting her to move South with him.

An immediate and unintentionally appalled no hadn't been the answer she'd wanted.

"Ah, well." Richard clapped David on the arm. "You're a young man with plenty of other options. And there's a lot to be said for the bachelor existence."

Yes, there was. David had led a rich and varied social life for the last few years, work permitting. He enjoyed women. Even if lately he'd been subconsciously comparing them to the one who had pushed him away.

"Lunch sounds good," David said, lifting his charcoal suit jacket from where it hung on the back of his chair.

"Excellent. I'll have Francine call ahead to get us a table at the club. Meet you in about an hour?"

That gave David just enough time to finish outlining a report he was supposed to summarize this week and maybe read a few e-mails. But after he'd returned to his office, all he could think about was his impending return to the land of peaches, bad traffic and sexy Southern women. He hadn't mentioned to his family that he might be moving back. He knew they'd be excited about his being just a few hours from home, and he'd wanted to wait until he knew for sure.

Now, he could tell them he was not only moving, but that before this time next year, he would quite probably take over as AGI's Vice President of Business Development. The current VP had lived in Boston his entire life and had no desire to relocate now, within a few years of retirement, whereas David was young, ambitious and had contacts in the southeast. The partners could have put the move in the hands of Richard Gunn, who would also eventually transfer to Atlanta, while Andrews and Innes remained in Boston running the technological development side of the company. But obviously they wanted to give David this chance to prove himself.

He savored the thought of announcing the promotion to his proud family. Much as he loved them, he reveled in the knowledge that they hadn't exercised any of their considerable influence to get him the position.

David *had* e-mailed Serena about the possibility of relocation, but in a vague, almost hypothetical way. When her "oh, that might be nice" response hadn't exactly denoted her jumping for joy in front of her computer monitor, he'd strategically dropped the subject. *I just didn't want to jinx my chances at the leadership role.* Not that he believed in jinxes...unless it was convenient.

He could call her now, he thought, as he glanced through his window at the soft rain that had begun to fall.

April showers were hardly rare (hence the popular term), and the undoubtedly chilly mist outside bore no resemblance to the summer deluge that had taken him and Serena by surprise. Still, considering the way she'd been crowding his thoughts since the news this morning, it didn't take much to bring that August downpour to mind.

They'd started the evening at an outdoor café in her eccentric neighborhood. Sharing a bottle of wine, they'd talked about being single, swapping progressively naughty anecdotes about their love lives before the unexpected storm sent them fleeing to her apartment, a renovated building that had once been a public school.

David had been sexually aware of her since he'd first seen her years ago arguing with someone in Student Affairs. But throughout their college friendship, which had begun while he briefly dated her roommate, one or both of them was usually involved with someone else, up until the time David had gone to Boston. Most of Serena's boyfriends—such as the current touring artist David had dubbed the Happy Wanderer—were David's polar opposites. So, when he'd spontaneously kissed her in her apartment, it had been without the usual Savannah Grant guarantee of getting what he wanted. He hadn't been absolutely one-hundred-percent sure she'd kiss him back.

But she had. And then some. She'd gone from a flirtatious friend he met for a few annual dinners to a blond siren with glinting brown eyes and a body like hot satin.

His memories played in digitized HiDef with surround-sound: the wanton invitation in her body as she'd reclined across that ridiculous purple couch of hers—a couch he hadn't been so inclined to mock the next morning—the glow of her ivory skin and the tiny gold navel ring illuminated by flashes of lightning. The feel of her beneath his hands and mouth as he'd conducted a slow, teasingly soft exploration in direct contrast to the urgently pounding rain on the roof above them.

It had been sexual nirvana, and when his plane had touched down the next day at Logan, he'd already been thinking about how soon he could get back to Atlanta—not that they'd discussed seeing each other again. They'd overslept, and he'd barely caught a cab in enough time to make his flight. Then he'd come home to that damn e-mail that professed her longstanding "affection" for him and ended with the insistence that they resume a platonic friendship.

Since her announcement that she'd started dating Happy, David had dated plenty, too. He'd had a good time, but he'd yet to reexperience the explosive chemistry he'd shared with Serena. He supposed they'd never know what would have happened if she hadn't been "too busy" to see him when he'd returned to Georgia for the holidays.

Now, he'd be returning permanently. David grinned at the possibilities. Yes, Serena was strong-willed and in a quasi-relationship. But David was a Savannah Grant, and judging by this morning's signs, he had to conclude the universe was on his side.

Had she reconsidered the platonic guidelines in the months since he'd last seen her? Did she think of their night together? How would the sexual innuendo that had crept back into their e-mails translate to a face-to-face meeting?

Only one way to find out.

SERENA DONAVAN'S computer screen displayed the spreadsheets for this month's income and expenses, but the information there was depressing enough that she was mostly staring out through the reception area's picture window into the tiled hallway. For a Friday, today had pretty much sucked. *Should've worn my lucky earrings.*

The two-room office suite with its eclectic furniture might not be posh, but the near-Buckhead address for her self-owned business wasn't cheap. She needed more lucrative offers than the earlier fraternity request, asking if she'd exchange her party-organizing services for beer—or, even less likely, for the amorous attentions of a post-grad who claimed he could ruin her for other men.

On the bright side, the slow business day meant her assistant's absence wasn't a strain, but it also meant reduced chances of a profit this month. Or electricity next month. Since Serena had to shell out money for caterers and deejays ahead of time, she was the one in a crunch if clients missed a payment or, in the case of this morning's thrilling news, bounced a check.

When the phone rang, Serena mentally crossed her fingers. She settled the headset behind her ear, summoning her optimism as she pressed the call-intercept button. Even another dead-end inquiry was better than her bank informing her that *her* account was being charged for someone else's insufficient funds. She'd have to ask her father, the southeast regional manager of a bank chain, about the logic behind that penalty.

"Inventive Events," she said with a smile, trying to infuse her words with the right blend of bold creativity and competitive pricing. "We party professionally."

"Hi." There was a pause before the warm male voice asked, "Serena?"

David.

Speaking of ruining a girl for other men…

"Hey." She blinked. "Long time, no hear." In the technical sense, anyway.

They kept up with each other, but not usually by phone. E-mail allowed her to write if she happened to be thinking of him at two in the morning, and helped him stay in touch despite his executive workload with a voice technology corporation. Or his ever-so-slightly less hectic schedule squiring around socialites.

Maybe she was just feeling grouchy about his dating because *her* most recent relationship had fizzled.

It suddenly occurred to Serena that the pause in their barely begun conversation bordered on awkward. "David?"

"Sorry," he said. "Hearing your voice threw me for a loop. I was expecting your assistant to answer, so when I got you, it caught me off guard."

"I gave Natalie the day off to nurse a broken heart," Serena explained.

"Softie."

The slight warble of cellular static didn't mask the grin in his voice. When she'd made the uncharacteristic decision to major in business—one of the few her father had ever approved of—no one had doubted she was smart enough to handle the coursework. But plenty had questioned whether or not she had the personality and killer instincts for it.

Her good-boss gesture, however, had been a purely selfish act of sanity preservation. Natalie saw her breakup, coming so soon after Serena's, as a huge potential for bonding. She refused to believe that Serena wasn't upset about being abandoned by Patrick…which she still hadn't mentioned to David. He'd teased her enough *during* her relationship with the celebrated sculptor who was wandering the country in a quixotic quest for inspiration.

I'll tell David about the breakup some other time, Serena rationalized, *when we're not on his dime.* Yeah, because a Savannah Grant ever worried about dimes. "So, to what do I owe the pleasure of this call?"

"Oh, the usual. Just wanted to ask what you're wearing."

She laughed, echoing his teasing tone and glib reply. "The usual. Leather pants and black bustier."

His appreciative wolf-whistle made her wonder where he was and if there were people in earshot speculating on his conversation. Clearly, David had ducked out a little early and wasn't stuck inside his office on a gorgeous spring day. Assuming it was gorgeous in Boston.

She spared a wistful sigh for the afternoon she could have had if she'd been irresponsible enough to play hooky. Tricia, the mother who had raised her in a modern-day art commune after the divorce, would have blown off work to spend the day "nurturing herself," but Serena had been influenced just enough by her father to keep her in the office today. He'd been so dedicated to work that his wife and daughter had seen him less and less each year.

Dismissing thoughts of her parents, she asked, "So, where are you calling from?"

"You're going to have to give me a minute. I'm still working on this visual," David drawled in a send-shivers-up-her-spine tone. In the sterile, black-and-white, Arial 12 e-mail format, their flirting was mostly benign, but when rendered in that husky voice…

"Okay," he said. "The real reason I called is to find out what you're up to this weekend."

"Th-this weekend?" Her pulse stuttered.

"Yeah. Too busy to see an old friend?"

If he'd been "thrown for a loop" when the expected receptionist hadn't answered, then Serena was now hurtling through the upside-down-and-back-again-lightning-curves equivalent of a new coaster at the nearby Six Flags.

Tell him you're working, dating, painting your apartment. Something, anything, lie! The problem was, she didn't have pressing plans, and while she had many faults—just ask her soon-to-be stepmother—dishonesty had never been one of them.

She pinched the bridge of her nose. "I don't have anything urgent on my schedule."

"Great! I thought we might get together."

A dozen vivid images burst to life behind her closed eyes, most of them featuring David in various states of undress. It had been months since they'd been together, but on that last visit, they'd *really* been together. In at least four different positions, come to think of it…which she tried valiantly not to do.

When he'd been in town during December, she'd used the event-filled season as an excuse not to see him, although they both knew she could have fit in a quick coffee if she'd wanted. The problem was, she'd wanted that entirely too much. She cared enough about David that an affair between them had the potential to really hurt her. Though she'd had her share of boyfriends, none of the eventual goodbyes had caused her any lasting emotional distress. But none of those boyfriends had been David.

When they first met, she'd considered him the attractive, if vaguely arrogant, guy one of her roommates dated. Later he'd gone on to become a fellow student in some "crossover" courses available to both under- and postgrads, to a study buddy it was fun to debate with, to the eventual friend she could e-mail on any topic from a commercial that had amused her to a painfully awkward reconciliation attempt by her father. David was now important enough to her to pose an actual threat to her heart. Especially if she lost him.

But how long could she brush him off without *that* becoming a threat to their friendship? Unless her brilliant plan was to avoid him forever, she had to get the first reunion out of the way.

She just wished he'd given her more time to prepare. Torn, she spun her padded green office chair in slow circles behind the receptionist's desk and debated. She and David were both experienced adults who had dated other people in the meantime. How potent could the chemistry between them still be?

His sigh ended the heavy silence. "You don't want to see me."

For a nonsensical second, she thought the crackling she heard was actually the tension between them. Then she realized he must be going through an area where reception was choppy.

"Does this have anything to do with your being with Happy now?" he asked. "Or is it because…?"

This one time, she didn't chide him over the nickname he persisted on using for Patrick, or the derisive note that crept into his voice whenever he mentioned her boyfriend. Ex-boyfriend. "Actually, there's something I wanted to tell you about H—him. We aren't seeing each other anymore." Not that she'd seen much of him when they *were*. A lot of Serena's relationships seemed to work that way.

David's pause was difficult to read, and it stretched on

long enough for her to wonder if he'd even heard her. Maybe the cell phone reception had given out all together.

But then he asked, "So you're single?"

Although his words went up at the end in a way that should have indicated a question, his self-assured tone made it sound as if he'd just proclaimed her available for the taking. When her tummy fluttered, caution warned this was exactly why she should avoid him again.

On the other hand, caution wasn't Serena's predominant trait. Besides, her pride balked at the thought of doing another ostrich impression like the one she'd performed in December. On the *other* other hand, at least he couldn't kiss her if her head was in the sand.

The man needed an answer, and she'd definitely run out of hands.

She took a deep breath. "I have a few things that need to be done this weekend, but if you're swinging through town, I'd love to get together for lunch—or coffee." Something midday and public and impervious to rain.

"Terrific." His next words distorted and faded completely before she heard, "Afraid you...too busy."

Only if she were smarter.

Footsteps sounded out in the hallway, and even though she'd probably see someone headed upstairs to the pricey orthodontist when she turned around, she seized the excuse to disconnect and regroup. "I've got a client coming in, so I need to run. Call me later with your itinerary."

As she spoke, the door behind her opened. Shocked to discover the footsteps really *had* signaled a business interruption, she whipped her chair around. And sucked in her breath at the sight of the dark-haired man smiling at her from the entryway.

"Or we could just talk about it now." David folded his cell phone, leaving her with the drone of the dial tone and a sudden absence of oxygen. His blue eyes, lighter and more intense than she remembered, slid over her still-seated body in unabashed appreciation, and he flashed a wickedly sexy grin. "It's good to see you, Serena, but damn, I was really hoping you were serious about the bustier and leather pants."

2

WORDLESS SHOCK immobilized Serena. How the devil had he become even *better* looking?

In retrospect, her earlier wondering about how potent the chemistry between them could still be was laughable. His voice on the phone had been enough to generate liquid heat inside her. Now she was faced with a mischievous expression as suggestive as the voice. His sensual lips—the bottom one just full enough for her to want to sink her teeth into it—were curved in a smile that crinkled his pale eyes at the corners. His body was tight, and he'd rolled back the cuffs of his midnight-blue shirt to reveal corded forearms. She had an image of those muscles straining as he held himself above her.

Losing the breath she'd finally managed to catch, she decided it wasn't such a hot idea to stare at his arms. Or his broad shoulders or his *very* nice hands.

"David!" She yanked off the phone headset and wondered absurdly what her short mop of hair looked like. There was no way she matched his flawlessly put-together appearance, not that something like that would have bothered her when they'd first met.

Back then, his dark-brown hair had been shaggier—not long, by any stretch of the imagination, but more tousled.

Each time she'd seen him since he'd earned his MBA, his hair had been trimmed a bit shorter. Now it was cut so close, you couldn't help but notice the strength of his rectangular face, the hard, smooth jaw and blunt, masculine features. His hair was just long enough for a slight upswept curve above his forehead and the barest hint of neat sideburns stopping at his ears.

"Surprised?" He shut the door behind him, still grinning that wouldn't-you-like-to-remove-my-clothes-with-your-teeth smile. Or maybe she was projecting.

"You rat." She stood, relieved she was able to, and pressed a palm to her racing heart. "I'm *shocked*. Why didn't you tell me you were here?"

His lithe easy stride as he came toward her made her feel melodramatically tense in contrast. "It was more fun this way. Besides, the Serena I know likes surprises. You aren't happy to see me?"

It was difficult to imagine anyone with David's self-assurance, heritage or bone-melting appeal worrying about the reception he'd get.

"Of course I am." Forcing her feet to walk around the soothing haven of Natalie's desk, Serena bobbed her head in what was supposed to be an affirming nod. Somehow she forgot to stop and ended up feeling like one of those ugly little dogs people stuck to their dashboards. "It's, um, been a while."

He said nothing, merely hitched an eyebrow in a knowing expression. The gap between visits had only been so long due to her sprouting a beak and feathers last time he'd been in town.

I'm not a chicken. Or an ostrich. Or anything else ornithological. She could hold her own against the waves of testosterone and sexual confidence he exuded. To prove just that, she stepped in his direction, stopping only when she was close enough for a quick, welcoming hug.

She wrapped one arm across his shoulders and leaned toward him. "It's great to see you."

His familiar cologne wafted over her, immediately calling to mind other earthy fragrances, like rain in the air and sex on her sheets. The memory was so strong that she froze for a second. David looped his arms around her waist, pulling her against him for a full-frontal hug, and her muscles went liquid with both recognition and anticipation.

Forget it, she instructed her body. There had been extenuating circumstances behind the one time they'd made love. Rather, the one night they'd made love many times. For starters, there'd been that whole wet clothing issue.

Still, while she had no intentions of repeating past mistakes, no matter how orgasmic, the man felt *good*.

Patrick had been long and lean—all right, gangly—and had towered over her in a way she'd tried to tell herself made her feel feminine. But David, just tall enough to grin down at her, was the perfect height. Their bodies fit together in all the right throbbing places.

Despite the fabric barriers of clothing, heat sprang from each point of contact as if the two of them were pressed skin to skin. Her breasts brushed against him, and her nipples tightened the same way they would have if they'd encountered the soft friction of the crisp hair that dusted his chest. His hips bumped hers, and a giddy, tingly sensation shot from head to toe as warmth pooled between her thighs.

Serena jerked back, which would have worked better if the contact with David hadn't dissolved her muscles. Without him for support, her strangely shaky body wobbled. She feared landing on her ass and looking like one.

"You okay?" He steadied her with a hand on her upper arm, his fingers firm through her thin violet sweater.

Goose bumps sprang up all over her flesh. As she recalled, the man had the most talented fingers this side of the Mason Dixon. She wasn't too shy to tell a lover where or how she wanted to be touched, but with David, there'd been no need. In fact, the few times she had volunteered a suggestion—*faster* came to mind—he'd continued his slow, sweet pace anyway, eventually demonstrating that he knew exactly what he was doing.

"I'm fine," she lied. "Just…light-headed."

She reclaimed her arm, expecting to see some kind of thermal handprint on her sleeve, burned into place by the heat arcing between them. "With Natalie out of the office, I didn't eat lunch." Unless she counted the salad she'd brought from home and the bag of chips from the vending machine. Fine, two bags, but they'd been the comparatively healthy baked-not-fried kind.

David's grin widened, and, with the clarity of hindsight, she immediately regretted her fib.

"Then I insist you let me take you out for an early dinner," he said.

"But—"

"I won't take no for an answer, Serena."

An occasionally stubborn person herself, she admired assertiveness in others, but the intimate timbre of his voice was downright unfair.

"I can't just dash off this second," she protested.

Actually, with the slow business day she'd had, she probably *could*, but why tell him that? David Grant could stand for a few more people to turn him down from time to time. She loved the man, she really did—in the nonphysical best-buds-for-ages sense—but he got his way much too often.

"I don't mind waiting," he said. "I can step out and make a few phone calls where the reception's better."

At the prospect of more space between them, her body sagged in relief. "All right. Give me a little bit to wrap things up."

"Take as long as you need." The corner of his mouth lifted. "Anything important enough to do deserves time and thorough attention, right?"

As the president of her own company—even if it was just her and one other employee—she should agree with the work ethic of his statement. Except there was no work ethic, only veiled seduction. She recalled again the way David had pushed her to mindless limits when she'd already thought she couldn't burn any hotter. He'd proven her deliciously wrong.

"You really do look woozy," David observed.

Of course she did. It had been months since she'd had sex, and close to a year since she'd had fantastic sex. Suddenly, it seemed every molecule in her body was vibrating with the effects of the unplanned abstinence. It was like alcohol—if you'd given up drinking for a while, even a sip of something potent went straight to your head.

His forehead wrinkled as genuine concern replaced the humor in his expression. "Are you sure you don't want to get out of here now and grab something to eat? Or I could run and get you a snack."

"No, that's not necessary." She glanced between the receptionist's chair and the overstuffed loveseat for guests, gauging which was closer. Deciding on the blue loveseat, she passed by David, telling herself she'd had a full five minutes to grow immune to that spicy seductive cologne. Its power over her should have waned by now.

Maybe the warm flush stealing through her body was actually embarrassment, not attraction. He was hardly the only man she'd ever been with, yet here she was in a near swoon. *Real women do not swoon.* Not in the last hundred years, anyway. When she glanced up, she was relieved to find him studying the surroundings instead of her.

"Nice place," he said. "Took me a while to find, but great location. Definitely an improvement."

Hard to believe her office would be terribly impressive to someone who'd grown up in the ancestral mansion once photographed for *Southern Décor,* but he was right about the improvement part. Her first site had been a one-room dive with a slight bug problem. Rent here was more, but worth every penny.

David took in the vintage lamp in the corner, the scarlet patterned swag over the miniblinded exterior window, the framed posters, and the artfully "mismatched" furniture—two chairs and a couch, each in a different primary color. "It is original."

"Thanks… That was a compliment, right?"

"Yeah." He sat next to her. "You have a way of making everything you come in contact with uniquely yours."

He wasn't crowding her, but then, he didn't need a macho tactic to make her aware of him. Some of her best memories with this man involved a couch, and she had to concentrate to keep from swaying reflexively toward him. As seemingly relaxed as she was alert, he leaned back and casually fanned his fingers against his knee. Was he *delib-*

erately drawing her attention to his hand, daring her to remember the way he'd touched her?

She swallowed. "Well, we do parties, so I didn't want my office to be stuffy. There are already wedding coordinators who do the whole Emily-Post-slash-Martha-Stewart thing, and planners all over the city who do the black-tie corporate banquets. We do those, too, but I try to give everything a touch of unique flair."

"Touch is good."

"W-we want our events to be memorable."

"You are that," he said softly. Just when she was starting to suspect he'd traveled all this way to drive her out of her sex-starved mind, he asked, "So, how's business going?"

It took her a moment to adjust to the change of subject. Oh, wait, they'd *been* talking about work. Outwardly, at least.

"Not bad. A little slower than I'd like right now," she admitted. "But business comes in waves. I arranged a bachelor party last week to fill some downtime."

"Bachelor party?" An eyebrow arched up. "With a stripper and everything?"

"She much prefers 'exotic dancer,' and I hired her through the same agency I contact for bartenders and black-jack dealers."

"Hm. An evening of sex, Scotch and sin, as presented by Serena Donavan."

"As presented by Inventive Events," she corrected, wishing the gleam in his gaze weren't quite so speculative. "Quit looking at me like you're picturing I was the stripper."

He leaned toward her, his smile naughty. "Do I have to stop picturing it, or just stop *looking* like I am?"

His husky tone seduced her into sharing the fantasy. It

was too easy to envision giving a sultry performance for
him alone—slipping buttons out of their holes, shimmy-
ing out of a blouse as she rolled her shoulders and hips to
the accompaniment of pulsing background music.

She narrowed her eyes. "You are a bad influence. Can't
you see I'm trying to be a respectable businesswoman here?"

Well, that wasn't entirely true. She'd been trying for
years to demonstrate that she didn't have to fit into her es-
tranged father's eight-to-five, corporate-America notions
of respectability to be happy and successful. The results
had been decidedly mixed—prompted in part by his new
girlfriend, James Donavan had decided last summer to try
to be part of her life again, but his brand of support included offers of finding her a job at one of his banks if "that
party thing ever falls flat."

Then again, how reputable could she be? She had strip-
pers on speed dial.

David shook his head, his tone laced with amusement.
"Give it up, Serena. You're not cut out to be respectable."

She flinched inwardly. David had teased her plenty of
times in the past and was only echoing what she herself
had just been thinking. Yet somehow the joking indict-
ment sounded a hell of a lot different coming out loud
from a Savannah Grant.

HOLDING HIS cell phone for prop purposes, David sat in the
lobby where "reception might be better," on a decorative
bench uncomfortable enough to have been used during the
Inquisition. Make a guy sit on one of these long enough,
he'd confess to just about anything. *Like being unbelievably
arrogant?*

AGI had sent him here this weekend to check out apartments, but David's personal goal had been to find out whether the burning attraction between him and Serena was as he remembered, or if his imagination and time had exaggerated it. He'd also wanted to discover if the Happy Wanderer presented any real competition. David's earlier call as he drove though an exasperating series of one-way Atlanta streets had eased his mind on both matters. Her announcement of the breakup and the breathy, telling pauses in conversation had led him to half hope she'd fall into his arms when he walked through the office door.

Arrogance.

Instead of fawning over him, or even pushing him away so he could tell himself she was running from a powerful desire, she'd blinked off her initial shock, then approached for a depressingly casual hug. If it hadn't been for the way she'd watched his hands while they talked on the couch, her doe eyes becoming heavy-lidded and dazed as if his fidgeting fingers were actually moving over her skin, he might honestly have worried that they were doomed to platonic friendship.

But the longer he'd sat with her, the more obvious her arousal had become. There'd been no mistaking her dilated pupils, the way she nervously licked her lips or the rapid rise and fall of her chest beneath her soft knit top. Maybe he'd only overlooked her desire at first because he'd been too consumed by his own.

Even though *he'd* been the one surprising *her*, when she'd glanced up at him with those wide brown eyes, the jolt of sensual energy that had shot through him had been like a force of nature—something meteorologists had warned was coming but that still had to be experienced to be believed.

For instance, who would have believed an ensemble as theoretically conservative as khakis and sweater could be so sexy?

Serena looked like a bad girl impersonating a business-woman. The slacks, while the right innocuous color for casual Fridays across the country, fit very snugly across her hips and were slung low at the waist. Only the embroidered hem of her plum-colored top kept him from seeing whether or not she was wearing the bellybutton ring that glinted teasingly in his memory. The neckline of the long-sleeved shirt dipped down in a rectangle that actually laced up over her breasts. Because of her understated curves, the cleavage revealed stopped just shy of being completely inappropriate for the office, but it was plenty to make his mouth go dry.

Although David knew it was an optical fashion illusion, he couldn't help thinking that if he pulled the ends of the string bow apart, her sweater would fall away and leave her bared for tasting. He could recall with aching clarity the feel of her velvety breasts and the peach-hued nipples that had been so sensitive to his touch. On the one occasion he'd undressed Serena, peeling off a sodden T-shirt that seemed to leave less to the imagination than actual nudity, she hadn't been wearing a bra. Was she today?

Wanting to find out had made him restless enough to drum his fingers and tap his thumb as he sat with her.

What he *really* wanted to find out was if she still objected to the physical connection between them. And if so, why. When he factored in everything that Serena meant to him, her newly single status and the timing of this transfer, it seemed fate was handing him this opportunity on a silver platter.

But Serena was on edge and clearly not about to fall into his lap—delightful as that prospect was. He needed to romance her, convince her, figure out her reservations and overcome them one by one. His desire to handle this with finesse was why he hadn't simply sprung his relocation announcement on her already. But he had supreme confidence that he could win her over. That was why he was on the business-development side of things at AGI—his specialty was new partnerships, finding or creating opportunities and overcoming any obstacles with various means of persuasion.

Persuading Serena would be far more enjoyable than, say, persuading the CEO of Digi-Dial, leaders in cell-phone technology.

Her office door swung open with a gentle creak, and Serena appeared, holding a massive beige purse that looked more like a weapon against muggers than something they might steal. In Boston, she would have needed a jacket, but it was warm here.

"Sorry I took so long," she said. Her tone was breezy and her smile even, but she ran her hand through her honey-blond, not-quite-chin-length curls in a self-conscious gesture.

"Not a problem."

She turned to lock up the suite. "If you'd like, I can suggest a place for dinner."

"Lord, no."

Serena was big on what she called "cultural color," and while four out of five places she picked were surprisingly excellent (with the fifth being horrific), David desired something a bit more intimate tonight. He didn't want their conversation to be interrupted by some poetry reading, and he didn't want to have to worry about exotic herbs in their un-pronounceable entrées that might lead to indigestion or unkissable breath. Just because he was prepared for longer-term wooing didn't mean he couldn't be optimistic.

"And what's wrong with the places I pick?" she asked, glaring down at him.

He stood. "They usually look like they're only still in business because someone bribed the health inspector."

"But they have fabulous food. Usually." She sniffed. "A restaurant doesn't have to have valet parking to be worth eating at."

"I know that." If his tone was defensive, it was because he'd just realized he'd been to at least three restaurants this week that used valet service. "But, tonight I want to take you...someplace nice." He could tell her they were celebrating his likely promotion, except he wasn't ready to tell her his news yet.

They headed toward the building's canopied main entrance. David reached out to open the door for her, but she'd already pushed it open herself.

Following her into the early-evening shadows, he felt a ridiculous need to prove she wasn't the only one who'd ever discovered a culinary treasure in an offbeat hole-in-the-wall. "There was a dive you would have loved in Boston."

"Meaning what?" She whipped her head around, impaling him with her narrowed eyes. "That I can only appreciate dives?"

Nice. Seduce women often, idiot? But he hadn't expected Serena to be so touchy.

"Meaning you would have seen beyond the unrefined décor, and you would have loved the live bands and the oyster bar's creative menu."

"Ah." On the sidewalk, she stopped, glancing between David and her dilapidated decade-old Honda.

Letting himself bump into her would have been transparent, but he came awfully close before he, too, drew up short. She'd never wear an expensive, trendy perfume, but whatever she had on smelled like spices and rare exotic flowers swirled in one heady, lust-inducing scent.

"Since you obviously don't need a recommendation from me, where *do* you want to go?" Serena asked.

To the nearest bedroom.

"In case we get separated in traffic," she added.

"Separated? We can ride together." In light of her apparent skittishness about spending time with him, he appealed to her time-honored sense of thrift. "I have to pay for the rental car whether we use it or not."

She sighed. "Let me guess, you're the Beemer over in the corner."

"Not even close." He gestured toward a sleek yellow convertible. "That's mine. Temporarily, anyway."

Her body tensed as she took in the sexy sports car, then she shot him a look of such unexpected disdain that he wondered if he'd have been better off with the BMW.

"Men. I suppose it was the flashiest one on the lot?"

The brightly colored fantasy on wheels had actually reminded him of Serena, but she didn't seem to be in the right mood to appreciate that compliment. "Well, it is yellow—"

"Extremely."

"—so I figured the pollen that coats everything here wouldn't show up as much." He shrugged when she didn't smile at the joke. "The weather's been dreary in Boston, and this looked like a great ride for the weekend."

"Looks expensive," she muttered. "What is it they say about men and cars and overcompensation?"

Without making a conscious decision to do so, he leaned forward, closing much of the space between them. "And what inadequacy do you think I need to compensate for?"

She blinked up at him. "None. It was a random comment. You…" As she trailed off, her eyes moved downward to the front of his pants, and her admiring gaze took what felt like his entire blood supply down with it. "Nothing inadequate about you."

Damn right. Still, he almost wished she'd challenged his prowess in some way. Then they could've skipped dinner, leaving him free to spend the rest of the night making his case.

3

Serena was sure someone, somewhere, had put a lot of time and thought into creating the right ambience for the restaurant, but the surroundings were wasted on her. She couldn't focus on anything outside of the intimate booth she and David shared.

The table for two was small enough that they could easily hold hands without having to reach for each other, not that they would be holding hands. Or touching each other at all, except for occasional accidents, such as his legs brushing hers under the table as they had just now. She almost jumped, her nerves taut with awareness.

His knee bumping mine is not *sexy.*

No, but the memories she had of their limbs intertwined beneath tangled sheets certainly were.

David leaned back against the richly upholstered bench opposite hers. "I know what I want. What about you, Serena?"

As with three-quarters of the comments he'd made on the drive to the restaurant, she couldn't tell if he intended his words to have a double meaning, or if she simply had a one-track mind. His tone was innocent enough, which in and of itself was immediate cause for suspicion.

"I haven't decided." The menu in its embossed burgundy

cover gave her something to hide behind when she worried her one-track thoughts would be revealed on her face.

After the time she'd taken in her office to adjust to his presence, the ride to the restaurant had been more relaxed than their initial encounter. His cologne was still driving her crazy—to say nothing of her preoccupation with his hands as he'd fiddled with the air vents and shifted gears—but she'd enjoyed being in his company. By the time he'd moved to Boston, they'd been friends long enough to have developed their own conversational rhythm, following each other's thoughts, knowing when it was safe to heckle the other about something and what subjects were more sensitive. So talking to him in the car hadn't been difficult. They'd discussed Inventive Events at length, and David's enthusiasm for her small but spunky business endeared him to her even further.

Now that she thought about it, her job had monopolized conversation, and she still wasn't clear on what work-related project had brought David to town. But, after dating an artist who was a minor celebrity in public opinion and a major celeb in his own, it had been gratifying for someone to show so much interest in what *she* did for a living. Her father, James, firmly believed there were more dignified ways to earn an income—ones that would probably reflect better on him—and certainly steadier incomes to be earned, given her education. Whenever Serena mentioned her company to him, he got a pained look on his face that she recognized from childhood.

It was the same one he'd always given her mom.

"Serena?"

She jerked her head up from a list of pasta entrées she hadn't been reading. "Still looking."

"No, I just wondered if everything was all right." David frowned. "You seemed...troubled."

"My mind wandered for a second. As seldom as I see James and Meredith, you had the bad luck to catch me on a week when I *have*." She knew her father was genuinely making an effort these days, but she'd honestly be glad when his early-June wedding to Meredith McPherson was behind them. With luck, he'd just go back to ignoring Serena. "Sorry. Guess not enough time's passed for me to have sufficiently detoxed from the visit."

"Oh." The lines of worry in David's expression eased. "That's a relief."

She raised an eyebrow.

"Not that I'm relieved by any trouble you're having with your family, just that I was concerned *I* might have upset you. I suddenly felt like maybe I'd strong-armed you into dinner."

Serena laughed. "You mean because you traveled across all those states, told me you wouldn't accept no for an answer and wouldn't even let me take my own car?"

"Is that all?" He flashed a grin. "It seemed worse in my head."

A moment later, he asked, "You want to talk about it? James and Meredith, I mean."

"No." She'd vented to David before, but not usually face to face. Besides, the last time she'd discussed her father with someone—her yoga-instructor friend Alyson—she'd ended up feeling whiny and disgusted with herself. "Big no."

David glided to the next logical topic. "Heard from Tricia lately?"

The mention of her adventurous, live-life-to-the-fullest mother made Serena feel surprisingly wistful, and she shook her head. "She and her latest lover, Miguel, are communing with South American nature far from the nearest modem or cell phone roaming area." Her mom, who hadn't had time to visit Serena in over a year, would have liked Patrick—they had the same respect for following "spiritual journeys." And the same inability to be there for someone else.

When the waiter arrived, Serena ordered a fettuccine plate. David, the carnivore, selected a New York strip.

"Very good." The waiter jotted down notes about side dishes and how to prepare the meat. "And you're sure you wouldn't like to see a wine list? We have a fabulous house chardonnay."

"Yes!...No." Serena was a bit too emphatic in her assurance, and she pretended not to see David's grin at her speedy response. "Yes, I'm sure that no, I don't need anything to drink."

They hadn't had nearly enough alcohol last summer to blame their indiscretions on impaired judgment, but the last thing she needed right now was something that lowered her already half-mast inhibitions. David's eyes alone triggered stabs of yearning in her. Would it really be so bad to ditch her inhibitions for the night? she asked herself as the waiter ambled to the next table.

Ending her dry spell with David, then sending him safely back to Boston with a quick kiss goodbye and a promise to stay in touch was tempting.

But dangerous, too. How willing was she to risk their friendship? Though she had friends, few had known her as long or as well as David. He was...special. Obviously her family wasn't ever going to be her main source of comfort and stability.

Newsflash, her libido informed her. *There's more to life than stability.*

Ignoring the way her inner muscles clenched whenever David happened to touch her, she reminded herself that one night together had already changed their relationship. Her powerful and conflicting emotions now were a perfect example. She didn't want things to unravel further. Among the many topics they discussed, she and David often mentioned their love lives, and before last summer, she'd never felt jealous. Well, hardly ever. But in the past few months, mention of that Tiffany person had given Serena far more of a twinge than had Patrick staying with an old girlfriend when he'd passed through New Mexico.

A self-sufficient woman, Serena did best in relationships where she and her partner could be alone together, as contradictory·as that sounded. Yet, when David had gone back to Boston after his last visit, she'd missed him. A lot. In an uncomfortably needy, vulnerable way.

So the answer to your question, she told her libido, *is yes. It would be* that *bad to ditch the inhibitions.*

She might not have many, but for tonight she was clinging to them. Even she—a woman who hadn't been with a man in months, a woman who had listened enviously to the erotic details of Alyson's tantric sex life—could keep her willpower intact for *one* night. With any luck, the next time Serena saw David she'd be safely involved with someone who had put an end to her sexual drought.

She set down the water she'd been sipping; her thirst wasn't what needed to be quenched. "So, what exactly brings you to Atlanta this weekend? I missed the specifics while we were trying to figure out where to turn."

"I saved the best news for last." He surprised her by

lightly brushing his hand over hers. Little pinpricks of heat shimmered up her arm. "You're looking at Atlanta's newest resident. AGI's moving its corporate headquarters here, and I'm heading up the advance team."

Moving? To her city? Within driving distance of her bedroom?

"Y-you aren't going back to Boston?"

"Well, yeah, temporarily. This is an exploratory visit. I'll be here through Tuesday, then go back to tie up all the loose ends. But after that, you may be seeing a lot of me."

Did she get to pick which parts?

Her willpower, which had been prepared for the demanding but blessedly short-lived sprint through a single intimate evening, now cramped at the thought of the endurance required for the long haul. She searched her mind for something that would help. "So…where does Tiffany fall on the 'loose ends' spectrum?"

His eyes widened. "Tiffany? Why would you ask about her?"

"Friendly curiosity. Isn't she your girlfriend?"

"That's a much more popular misconception than I realized," he mumbled. "No, she isn't. She apparently thought she was. Until she left me earlier this week."

"You were ditched by someone you weren't even dating?" Serena chuckled. "And I thought *my* getting dumped was pathetic."

"Dumped? You're kidding. I assumed you finally called things off because you were tired of carrying on an exciting affair with postcards."

He made a good point. Why hadn't *she* ended the going-nowhere relationship?

Patrick possessed a fair amount of charisma, but that

had been wearing thin even before he'd left town. She'd been philosophical about her lack of enthusiasm, though. None of the men she'd spent time with in the last nine months had caused much *zing* inside her. Without meaning to, without even realizing it until after the fact, she'd fallen into the dating equivalent of, "Why change the channel? Nothing else good is on."

David leaned back as the waiter set down their plates, then asked as soon as the man walked away, "What did happen, exactly? With you and the Wanderer?"

"He was searching for inspiration. Apparently, it's in Yuma." She twirled pasta around her fork. "He's staying."

"I thought this whole roving-the-country thing was a chance to—help me out here?"

"'Soak up myriad experiences and settings and return triumphant, synthesizing them into his work,'" she recited.

"Uh-huh. So, no synthesizing?"

Was it too late to tell the waiter she'd changed her mind about having a drink? "Yes. He'll just be synthesizing in Yuma. He told me I was welcome to visit him, but Atlanta was 'asphyxiating his art.'"

David's lips twitched. "It can breathe in Arizona?"

"I hear they have good air there."

He focused intently on his plate while he cut his steak into tiny pieces, all the while biting hard on his lower lip.

"Oh, just get it over with," she ordered, fighting a giggle herself. "Go ahead and laugh."

He did.

"Don't get me wrong, I'm sure he's a gifted artist," David said, more magnanimous than he'd ever been when she was actually dating Patrick. "Lousy boyfriend, though. I never could figure out why you stayed with him."

That was par for the course—David hadn't exactly been drinking buddies with anyone she'd dated. The reverse was also true, though. From the preppie ex-prom queen Student Housing had placed Serena with to the string of cool blondes from family money she'd watched David date, most of his romantic choices made her cringe. Did he really have fun with those women? Come to think of it, he was probably asking himself the same thing about her and Patrick.

How could she explain that in some selfish way, the absentee relationship had been ideal? She'd been able to combat loneliness by being "involved," yet she'd never had to give up her side of the bed. She hadn't even shaved her legs unless she felt like it.

She shrugged. "My line of work, I'm pretty busy during the prime weekend dating hours, so I didn't mind his being gone that much. I could call him if I needed to talk and still got gifts on my birthday and major holidays. Few of the hassles of a normal relationship, all the benefits. Except fantastic sex."

David set down his fork and studied her for a long, electric moment. The humor they'd shared evaporated beneath the heat in his gaze. "You know, Serena, there are guys who could give you the friendly ear, birthday cards and space to do your job...*and* the fantastic sex."

Her willpower whimpered.

DAVID'S provocative words were still fresh in Serena's mind when she woke up bright and early Saturday morning. Well, not "woke up," exactly, since that implied she'd actually fallen asleep sometime during the steamy night. Steamy partly because of her own thoughts, and also because when she'd tried to turn on the air-conditioner for the first time this season, she'd discovered it didn't work. Good thing she'd turned down David's request to see her home—what heat *that* would have generated!

After he'd taken her to pick up her car, he'd asked if she was sure she didn't want him to follow her home. His gesture, though sweet, was totally unnecessary. She might not live in the most upscale part of town, but it wasn't dangerous. Not nearly as dangerous as risking his being near her apartment or her ever-weakening willpower.

Which begged the question—why had she agreed to his picking her up here this morning?

Light spilled through the arched window at the other end of the loft's railing, and she blinked, wondering how he'd talked her into helping him apartment hunt.

He'd lulled her into a false sense of security, she told herself as she stood under the revitalizing spray of the shower. During dinner, his sexually charged comments had tapered off just enough so that when he'd announced that he'd naturally want her input as an Atlanta resident while he shopped for apartments, she'd agreed.

Did he really catch you so off guard, or were you just happy for the excuse to spend more time with him?

Ignoring the skeptical inner voice, Serena worked her blue cypress bar into a lather and ran it over her skin. The natural soap was supposed to be soothing to body and spirit, but after a sleepless night of rebellious fantasies and aching memories, she too easily imagined David's hands running over her slick body instead of her own. His wet fingers slipping along the curve of her hip, the smooth slide of her thigh... With a tight groan, she flipped the faucet control to Cold and rinsed quickly before pulling back the shower curtain.

If he could resume their friendship with no signs of awkward unease, so could she. In fact, keeping their relationship platonic was *her* idea. She couldn't risk the possibility of ruining their friendship, no matter how badly she'd wanted him last night and still did this morning.

Sure, opposites attracted. Notice how there was no equally famous saying about opposites settling down and living happily ever after. James and Tricia had demonstrated *vividly* what happened when two very different people moved beyond the attraction and into the bitter divorce stage. Although there had been painful times when Serena's parents had used their daughter as a weapon to hurt each other, at least she could take comfort in knowing she'd learned from their mistakes. The mere possibility that her friendship with David could one day end with the same sort of spiteful contempt as her parents' marriage made her stomach clench in dread.

But she knew he was interested in being more than buddies.

When she'd first e-mailed him to say their making love had been a one-time fluke, he hadn't seemed thrilled with her decision. Given his history of persevering until he got what he wanted—whether it was a class schedule with every course he'd desired to the most sought-after girl on campus to his number-one job pick—Serena wouldn't have been surprised last night if he'd pushed her to change her mind. Instead, he'd made comments, such as the remark about her finding a man who could take care of her sexual needs as well as her emotional ones, but then he'd moved to safer topics.

By the time he'd driven her back to her car, she was almost wishing he'd just address their single night together directly so she had reason to reiterate her never-gonna-happen-again stance. But he hadn't broached it, and she wasn't about to bring it up first. Not when it was taking everything in her to keep it from happening again.

She ran a towel over her hair in a cursory gesture that wouldn't really do anything to keep it from drying in whatever wild curls it chose. Serena actually liked it that way. She couldn't imagine the time and care Alyson took plaiting her long red hair in all those elaborately braided styles. Besides, when your hair was already messy, you never let the threat of disarray keep you from enjoying something like the breeze off a lake or an afternoon jaunt in a convertible with the top rolled down.

Dressed in a pair of pink capris, an oversized T-shirt covered in sketched portraits by a local artist and a pair of vintage sandals, Serena headed downstairs, her heart rate accelerating as she realized David would be here soon. She'd told him that management offices for most places wouldn't open until nine, but he'd insisted on buying her breakfast first to thank her for giving up her Saturday.

Certainly helps save on groceries. The free meals came at a fortuitous time. With the recent lull in business, it was nice to have dinner out without worrying about funds, but it was a forcible reminder that she and David lived different realities. It wasn't just the finances, though, or their up-bringings; they moved in opposing cultural circles. He went to the opera, she went to local bars to hear her struggling guitarist friend. David had gone for his MBA with the determination to make even more of himself than his birthright gave him, and Serena had studied business to get a good idea of what the rules were before she broke them.

When he'd kissed her last summer, she'd been stunned.

There'd always been the occasional flirtatious undercurrent to their conversations, but until that day and the surprising sparks that had combusted between them, she hadn't truly thought he was attracted to her. Romantically, they didn't make sense. As friends, he could tease her good-naturedly about the artistic way she'd decorated her various apartments because he didn't have to live in any of them, and she could cluck her tongue over the hellacious hours he worked because she wasn't one of the girlfriends he cancelled on to do so—she'd had enough of that on the weekends her father was supposed to take her, thank you very much.

Even without the excruciating ordeal of her parents' divorce, Serena had enough sense to know she wasn't David's type. That Tiffany he'd started mentioning a few months ago sounded perfect for him. *Yes, but she's in Boston, and they broke up. You are here with David.*

The knock at the door was a merciful interruption. She might be spending the day with David, but only because she was doing a favor for a friend. No different than spending a day with Alyson.

Except she didn't fantasize about Aly.

She crossed the hardwood floor, away from the windows and toward the door that opened into what had once been a junior-high hallway. In the part of the building where they'd housed the management offices, there were still some of the original lockers.

"Morning." David greeted her with a smile and a white paper sack that emanated delicious aromas. He looked even more delicious.

"You brought breakfast."

"I told you I was going to," he answered, shifting his

weight from foot to foot, as though wondering why he was still standing in the hall.

"Yes, but I thought…" Crowds, onlookers, public ordinances against her ripping off his long-sleeved red T-shirt and Dockers. She really, *really* needed to talk to the super about fixing her air-conditioning. "I'm sorry, come in."

He entered, but didn't head for the green-and-rose kitchen that sat below her loft-style bedroom at the other end of the apartment. Instead, he paused, glancing at her with those unbelievable sky-blue eyes. "I hope you don't mind my making a unilateral decision, but I saw that breakfast burrito vendor you liked so much was still in business and figured it would be a fun surprise."

"You are just full of those," she muttered.

His gaze held hers. "You aren't exactly predictable yourself, Serena."

Was he referring to the fact that they'd made love, or the fact that she was adamantly opposed to it happening again? Less adamantly every second that passed, she admitted to herself. Her body had remained in a ripe, sensitized half-aroused state ever since he'd set foot in her office yesterday, and now she wondered if she would have made things easier on herself if she'd tried to alleviate some of this building pressure when she'd been in the shower. Too late now.

Unless she asked him to help alleviate it.

She swallowed, then jerked her thumb over her shoulder toward the forest-green countertop of the breakfast bar that served as a room divider. "I—I have juice in the fridge. I might even have some coffee."

He grimaced, but his gaze was still affectionate. Heatedly so. "No offense, but your coffee's horrible. I grabbed some on the way over."

Pivoting on the blocky high heel of one sandal, she told herself she'd scarf down her food and get them out of here.

David followed at a slower pace, taking in the surroundings. "You've changed some stuff."

"Here and there. I wanted some new decorative touches, but the major furniture's all the same." Good thing she was skilled at creatively redecorating on a budget. And the orange-framed acrylic pieces she had on display not only livened up the high white walls, they allowed her to help her friend Craig without it seeming too much like charity.

"Glad to see you still have the couch," David told her, his voice husky with remembrance.

She froze reaching for juice, caught between the heat of her own memories and the welcoming blast of cold air that came from the fridge. Even now, every moment she and David had spent together that night was as vivid as her favorite Matisse painting—they'd barely shut the front door behind them when David had pulled her into that first startling, sizzling kiss. Then, when they'd managed to shimmy out of the majority of their sodden clothes, they'd made it as far as the bright purple velour sofa.

She struggled for a light tone, not daring to look out in his direction. "Oh, come on. You always made fun of that couch."

When he spoke again, his voice was so close, she jumped. "I've developed a new appreciation for it."

Straightening fast enough to give herself a head rush, she clutched the gallon of orange juice to her and leveled a reproachful glance in his direction. "You startled me."

"Sorry." He grinned. "I didn't exactly tiptoe in here, so you must've really been lost in thought."

The tiny room that she'd decorated to be evocative of a garden was nowhere near big enough for her, David *and* her peace of mind.

"If you want to have a seat," she suggested, "I can bring the juice out."

He took a step—in the wrong direction—and shrugged. "I like being in here."

Leaning past her, bringing his body so close it almost brushed hers, he stretched up to open the cabinet over her shoulder and pulled down two glasses. Serena held her breath, paralyzed in front of the refrigerator, mesmerized by how easy it would be to touch him. To live out the fantasy she'd been craving for the past nine months.

He set the glasses on the counter and lowered his voice. "I like being with you."

His words warmed her more than they should have, and she closed her eyes for a second as she stole a guilty moment to savor the sentiment. When he'd last been here, she'd not only *liked* being with him, she hadn't been able to get enough of him. She'd never been so insatiable with any lover, before or since. Would it still be that way between them?

Almost as if she'd asked the question aloud, he groaned in response. Serena felt him take the juice out of her hand and heard it land on the counter with a dull thud.

"Serena." The warmth of his breath was soft on her face, and he ran his thumb along the curve of her lower lip, skin so sensitive the caress almost tickled. It was all she could do not to catch the pad of his thumb with her teeth. "Look at me, honey."

Forgetting to breathe, she did as he asked, knowing he was about to kiss her. Wanting him to kiss her. She'd spent hours thinking about this very thing—not just during her hot sleepless night, but ever since he'd flown back to Boston last summer.

His gaze melted with hers, and he sucked in his own breath, his expression almost one of agony. Maybe he was afraid she'd push him away. As if that were even possible. Her entire body was starving for him.

She laced her fingers behind his neck and pulled him to her. His lips met hers eagerly, and the moment his tongue slid into her mouth, she felt dizzy with joy. *This* was what she'd longed for. This was what she'd remembered, what had kept her awake on nights she should've been missing Patrick but hadn't.

A small voice trying to be heard over the rush of desire warned, *this* was what was going to break her heart.

4

DAVID'S FINGERS were tangled in the damp softness of Serena's hair, and his thoughts were tangled in the overpowering desire that had snared him as soon as she'd opened the front door.

As sexually frustrated as he'd been when he got back to his hotel room last night, he'd known he'd handled dinner the right way, always retreating before his flirting went too far. Changing Serena's mind about this platonic nonsense required finesse, which had clearly been shot to hell the moment he'd set foot in this apartment. There'd been no misinterpreting the way she'd looked at him with those hot brown eyes. He'd been overwhelmed by the need in her expression, the fresh, exotic scent of her, the memories of the last time he'd been here.

Winning her over slowly was overrated. New plan: kissing her passionately.

Her hands skimmed up and down his back, bunching the material of his shirt and raking over his tensed muscles. He slid his own hands along the curve of her spine past her waist, kneading her round hips with his fingers as he pulled her against him. Her tongue met his, and hunger reverberated through him with the force of a tsunami.

There was no way to deepen the already carnal kiss, but

he could bring them closer together, eliminate the barriers between them. Gripping the hem, he shoved her pale purple shirt upward. He brushed over the delicate gold navel ring that had shimmered in his memories, and his erection swelled to almost painful proportions. Unlike in his memories, she was wearing a bra today, but the frothy scrap of lace could hardly be described as an obstacle. He ran his palm over her, and she moaned her approval, arching into his hand. He wanted to fill his hands with her, wanted to fill her, period.

He lifted her shirt, and she raised her arms so he could remove it. But with their kiss broken, she blinked up at him like someone waking from a trance. When he settled his arms back around her, she sighed his name.

"David." It wasn't so much rapturous desire as wistful regret.

Hell.

He stared into her eyes. "You don't want me to kiss you?"

She bit her lip, her face flushed the same rosy pink as the bra he'd love to slide off of her. Though she didn't answer, the tightness of her hold on him was encouraging.

"To touch you?" He traced his index finger in a slow circle around one silk-covered nipple. Maybe he wasn't playing fair, but he was playing to win. They were fantastic together—he just had to persuade her of that.

"I, um…" She swallowed convulsively. "Damn, it's hot in here."

It wasn't the room. It was all her. He reached behind her and cupped his hand under the ice-maker, then lifted a crescent-shaped cube to the back of her neck. Catching a handful of honey-blond curls and twisting them up off her nape, he drew the ice down over her skin. "Better?"

Not even the frigid droplets of water dripping between his fingers could quell the heat spreading in his body. Only Serena could put out that fire. He trailed a wet, shivery path across the top of her shoulder and down over her collarbone. She trembled, her eyes closing as her head tilted back. Tracing the rapidly melting piece of ice back and forth over the slopes of her small, perfect breasts, he fumbled one-handed with the clasp at her back. He'd seen her in his imagination a hundred times since August, but that only intensified his need for the reality.

The bra fluttered to the floor, but he didn't touch her immediately. He made them both wait, drawing a cold, slippery, straight line down her flat abdomen. Then, he changed direction, traveling up the column of her throat, dipping the ice across her parted lips. He pitched what was left of the cube into the sink behind them and bent to kiss away the cold.

She whimpered into his mouth, meshing her hands in his hair, and sucked on his tongue, greedy for him in a way that decimated his self-control. All he wanted in the world was to bury himself inside her. He settled temporarily for stroking his thumbs over her hard nipples in quick, insistent caresses as he kissed her neck.

Shifting her weight for balance, she bent her right leg up around his hip. Serena's flexibility was enough to make a grown man weep with joy. Cupping her backside, he pressed her closer as they kissed. He couldn't stop himself from moving against her, and she ground her own hips to meet his. As he reached for the zipper on her pants, he realized she was tugging at his clothes, too. He didn't have the remaining strength and coordination to support them both and explore her with the thoroughness he desired. Shrugging out of his shirt, he pulled her down to the smooth, cool surface of the linoleum floor with him.

Her capris remained on, but were loose around her waist as she lay on her side. With one arm around her, he nudged her to her back, finally in a position to lavish her breasts with hungry attention. He sucked on one engorged tip, then switched sides as he slid a hand down inside the silky confines of her panties. And then into the hot silky confines of *her*.

She was so wet. He brushed his fingers against her damp, swollen flesh, easily moving in and out of her, and the intimate knowledge of just how aroused she was spurred him to a more frantic pace. Before he fully comprehended what was happening, her soft, breathy murmurs became a wordless cry and she stiffened against his hand, her body bucking with small, silent ripples.

He'd had no idea she was so close. The intensity of her reaction was a marvel—making him feel powerful and humble and protective. He hugged her to him, partly to give her a moment to catch her breath, partly to express some of the wordless emotion that had swelled inside him.

She buried her face into his bare chest. "That... I don't normally— It's been a while."

Hypocritically pleased as he was by the fact she hadn't done this any time recently, his male pride was still a little pricked by her reasoning. Her exploding in his arms was not due to a dry spell, dammit, it was the chemistry between them. The perfect way to prove that would be to bring her to a second orgasm now, when she could no longer claim a sex-starved body.

But she didn't give him that chance. She was already

scooting away, her gaze darting around the kitchen, most likely seeking her discarded shirt. *Damn, damn, damn.*

"Serena." Short of imploring her to change her mind, he wasn't sure what to say. Not to mention his body was aroused to such a frustrating degree he was having a hard time speaking. Pun intended.

But along with the receding passion in her dazed expression, he saw confusion and vulnerability. The last thing he'd wanted was to upset her—he'd only been trying to convince her there was something between them. Something potent.

The tiny frown lines puckering her forehead sliced across his heart. She looked lost. He clenched his fists at his sides to keep himself from reaching for her again.

"I'm sorry." Her words were almost a sob as she clutched her shirt to her front. "That was incredibly selfish of me. I shouldn't have allowed things to get so carried away when I never intended to let them... I didn't mean to do that to you."

"It's not that you owe me anything, Serena. I enjoyed that as much as you did." He gritted his teeth against the discomfort of uneased need. "All right, maybe not *as* much, but I touched you because I wanted to. And because it was what you wanted." For reasons he still didn't get, she was reluctant to admit it.

She zipped her pants as she rose, then shrugged into her shirt. He wondered if it was pathetically simple-minded of him that for the rest of the day he'd be thinking about the fact she had no bra on underneath.

He stood, too. "Help me understand this. If you didn't want me, I could accept that with no problem. But—"

"Could you really?" Ducking away from his gaze, she

poured a glass of juice. "You always go after what you want. And you tend to get it."

He was both successful and determined, but he didn't bully people. And he didn't see what this had to do with them. "Don't tell me this is your way of helping me build character through rejection or something."

"Of course not." She scowled in his direction. "It's my way of prot— We're a bad match."

When he would have pointed out recent experience indicated otherwise, she cut him off with a warning glare.

"Okay," she relented. "In *bed* we're a pretty good fit."

In the most literal sense. She'd been exquisite around him. David bit back a groan at the erotic memory.

"But you've been part of my life for years, and I don't want to lose you." A very real vulnerability underlined her words, softening his ire.

Sex didn't have to mean loss. Sex was a good thing.

Unable to resist touching her for just a moment, he brushed his palm over her cheek. "I don't want that, either. But I don't see why—"

"Take a look around you! You grew up in a mansion and have relatives on Capitol Hill. I live in a converted school outside Little Five Points. My best friends are an unemployed artist and a yoga instructor, and I buy my formalwear at a vintage dress shop."

Was that all?

He was so relieved he almost laughed. "So? We aren't exactly living in Victorian times. The classes are allowed to intermingle freely now."

Her eyes narrowed. "Nice. I tell you how I'm feeling, and you make light of my valid concerns."

Whoops.

He'd already pushed too hard with that kiss-spun-wildly-out-of-control, and he didn't want to alienate her completely. If money was what was bothering her, though, surely he could make her see it wasn't an issue.

"I didn't mean it like that, Serena. I only meant it's not a problem." He'd always been aware of the advantages of being a Savannah Grant—a little *overly* aware, as evidenced by his zeal to succeed on his own capabilities—but he didn't judge people who were from a different background.

"Really? Because in case you hadn't noticed, the women you date tend to be polished blondes with trust funds."

Well, that was true. But he couldn't believe his bohemian friend was the one hung up on material issues. At a loss, he fell back on the years' long habit of joking with her. "You're blond. The rest we can work around."

"I don't want to work around it. I don't want this," she added, gesturing between the two of them with her hand.

The hell she didn't.

His immediate reaction was so vehement that it startled him. Was she right about him being too used to getting his way? No, that had nothing to do with his annoyance. He'd never had this kind of connection with another woman, and what bothered him was knowing she felt it, too, yet was dismissing it.

"Serena—"

She balled up a hand on her hip. "You were right about my not owing you anything. I don't have to justify this decision to you."

He expelled his breath in an angry gust and tried to recall the definition of *finesse*.

"No, you don't," he agreed slowly. "I guess I was just

hoping you'd changed your mind about that night being a mistake."

"I haven't." Her near-whisper was apologetic. "But if you've changed *your* mind about wanting me to apartment-hunt with you today, I'd understand."

Her expression was so forlorn, he wasn't sure whether he wanted to hug her or shake her.

"Is that really what you think of me? I just got finished agreeing our friendship is important to me." He sent her a reproachful glare. "I didn't stop valuing your opinion just because you don't feel like having sex."

"Oh." Biting her lip, she shrank into herself, looking both relieved and embarrassed. "Sorry."

He nodded, needing to get out of this apartment and away from the temptation of touching her again. "Let's just have our breakfast, and go see what we can find out there."

"Deal. And…maybe you could put your shirt back on now?"

He hid a grin at the wistful peek she stole in his direction. She might not *want* to be interested, but she was. He could work with that.

THE BUCKHEAD CONDO was okay, but the amenities were sub par, and David was developing a strong dislike for the property agent showing them the place. The woman with the tightly buttoned suit and even tighter bun had given Serena a rather condescending smile earlier, following her disapproving double take at Serena's avant-garde shirt. David hadn't even realized until seeing the woman's pinched expression that several of the people drawn onto the pale purple cotton were nude. They blended into the sea of portraits.

Besides, he'd been far more fixated on the naked form *beneath* the shirt, though he'd tried to rein in his lust to put Serena at ease. She'd been stiff and tense when they first drove away from her place—why the hell hadn't he stuck to his slow and steady plan?—but she'd gradually relaxed to her usual self over the last couple of hours. Still, as he'd listened to Realtors chirping on about ceiling fans and furnished washers and dryers, he kept coming back to Serena's earlier anxiety. It floored him that a woman with her gusto and unconventionality could be so wary of taking a chance on—

"Mr. Grant?" The bun-woman was speaking to him, her tone resolute as she tried to close the deal. "As you can see, this unit is top-notch. I doubt it will be on the market long. Would you like to take a few more minutes to look around while I start up the paperwork?"

"Thank you, but I don't think that will be necessary," he said pleasantly. "This one's not quite what I'm looking for."

The woman sniffed and spluttered her disbelief as he and Serena showed themselves to the door.

"So what were your objections?" Serena asked as they crossed the parking lot. The spring breeze billowed her shirt, then flattened it for a moment to the body he was trying so hard not to think about. "David? You didn't like it, right?"

What was not to like?

The apartment, idiot.

He forced himself to focus. "The space was okay, but there are zero perks to living here and the parking's lousy. Why, did you think I should've considered it?"

"Uh-uh. Lousy natural light, negative energy. I hated it, I'm just trying to get a feel for what specifics matter to you." She buckled her seatbelt. "I got a bad vibe off the place."

He laughed. "A vibe? Tell me that's not how you're going to help me decide where to invest my hard-earned money. What about real-estate appreciation and property resale values?"

"Resale?" She blinked at him. "Sorry, I guess I've been a little, um, distracted today. You aren't planning to rent?"

"No. You didn't hear me talking to bun-lady about that?"

"I tried to be wherever she wasn't. Talk about negative energy."

Well, they agreed on that. "I realize not everyone can afford to buy a place, but since I can, why throw money down the drain every month?"

He worked long hours and didn't want to tack on additional time for a commute to a home outside the city. But that didn't mean he wanted to pay an exorbitant rent with nothing to show for it. Judging by the way Serena was staring at him and shaking her head in disbelief, his luxurious housing budget wasn't helping allay her concerns about their disparate statuses. Did she honestly think that the cost of monthly rent was a reason not to explore what simmered between them? Hell, she'd tolerated the obnoxious wandering artist and *his* many quirks.

David had seen her date all kinds of guys, and he found it somewhat bewildering she wouldn't at least give him a chance. Had she e-mailed any of those guys for moral support when her father had called after all these years to say he was dating someone new and wanted Serena to meet her? Did those other guys know that her guilty secret her junior year of college was a serious "Days of Our Lives" addiction? Did they know which pair of turquoise teardrops were her "lucky earrings," that she made the worst coffee known to mankind but an incredible stuffed eggplant dish he'd been reluctant to try and had fully expected to hate?

Serena fidgeted in her seat. "Thinking about what you want in a place?"

"Not exactly." More like what she wanted in a man. Why wasn't he it? "But thank you for coming with me. I know I didn't give you much notice, and you could've been doing other things today."

"Anything for a friend," she said lightly.

He knew this was true—Serena was both loyal and incredibly soft-hearted—but he also picked up on the understated emphasis she used on *friend*. She might as well have said "anything for someone I have no intention of sleeping with." Maybe she didn't, at the moment, but maybe his moving to Atlanta would give him the opportunity to change that.

5

As Serena unlocked her office Monday morning, she realized she was in serious need of a plan B. When she'd gone to dinner with David Friday evening, her game plan had been simply to resist him. Resist those gorgeous blue eyes and the way they focused on her when she was talking, resist his sexy grins and sexier kisses, resist her own body's insistence that no man would ever make her burn like this again... Of course, not even twenty-four hours after he'd hit town, he'd been undressing her on her kitchen floor.

So much for the "resist" approach.

She sorted through the weekend mail that had been left in her box, but she kept seeing David's face instead of the four-color brochure for a new company specializing in novelty ice sculptures. Plan B began to take shape—a buffer. She needed help, and she wasn't above drafting some for the lunch she and David had scheduled for today.

When he'd taken her home Saturday, no closer to finding an apartment than he had been that morning, she'd had excuses ready for why she couldn't spend Sunday with him, too, but he hadn't asked. Instead, he'd only wanted to know if she could spare a lunch hour to say goodbye on Monday before he left town early Tuesday. That had sounded safely platonic.

But after spending all yesterday regretting that she hadn't invited David in to finish what they'd started Saturday morning… Safe? Platonic? Hadn't she ever heard the term *nooner?*

Oh, yeah. No way was she going to lunch alone with him.

Five minutes later, Natalie Harris, the answer to Serena's problem, sashayed in the door, with a defiant look-at-me-I-don't-need-a-man bounce in her step.

Serena had witnessed Natalie post-breakup before. First came the grieving, which had probably included a crying jag and a DVD weekend full of rented tearjerkers. This was followed by her confident-woman, I'd-rather-be-single-anyway, denial. Then came the brunette's man-killer rebound stage, in which she decided she *did* want men…as long as she could love 'em and leave 'em.

After all that, there was usually a two-week period of actual emotional stability before she met her new future boyfriend and the cycle started over from the top (single-minded infatuation and practicing how his surname would sound hyphenated with hers).

"Hey." Natalie dropped a leopard-print handbag on her desk. It went well with her black short-sleeved sweater dress and the leopard-print scarf she'd tied sarong-style at her waist. "Have a nice weekend?"

"Not bad." Serena stood in the doorway of her office. "What about you? How're you holding up?"

"Great." The receptionist was fairly convincing as she measured out coffee for the machine they kept in the corner. "I was finished crying by Friday night and took myself out shopping Saturday. Got a new purse."

"I noticed. Pretty spiffy."

"And some *fabulous* clothes on sale. They look great on me. Men will just have to watch me walk by and eat their hearts out." Natalie tossed her head in a disdainful gesture, rippling her long dark hair. "Because I am not going down that path again. What do I need a guy for?"

"Absolutely nothing," Serena said in the expected show of solidarity.

"That's right." Natalie lifted the empty coffeepot in salute. "We are women. We are strong."

Well, they were women.

And maybe Natalie was strong.

But Serena and her fragile willpower made eggshells look indestructible.

"What's wrong?" Natalie asked, her hazel eyes narrowing as she studied her employer. "This is about Patrick, isn't it? The shock has worn off and you've finally realized you're alone. Oh, doll, you shoulda called me over the weekend. We could've shopped together."

Patrick? Serena laughed weakly. He hadn't even crossed her mind in the last twenty-four hours. "No, I'm over him. Really."

The fact that the breakup had left such a minimal impression on her was probably significant. Was it possible she'd been over him even when she was *with* him? She bit her lip, wondering guiltily if part of the sculptor's appeal had been the added barrier between her and David after their one-night stand.

No, that was ridiculous. Patrick had been an artist with admirable vision, someone who shared common pastimes and sensibilities with Serena and her circle of friends. Besides, she and David had already had the barrier of a thousand miles between them. She didn't have to stoop to using someone as a human shield.

"Hey, Natalie, what are your lunch plans today?"

SERENA SAT in the back seat of the sleek yellow convertible, trying not to be miffed at her own ingenuity. After David's initial moment of surprise in her private office when she'd asked if Natalie could join them for lunch, he'd agreed with a knowing smile.

So *infuriatingly* knowing that she'd blurted, "And it's not because I don't want to be alone with you, either!"

His grin had widened. "Did I say that?"

"You remember I mentioned her recent breakup? Well, I didn't want to leave her here all by herself when she could be out with us, trying to have fun again. I'm, um, worried about her."

David had glanced over his shoulder through the window that looked into the main reception area, where Natalie smiled and flirted with the UPS man. "Yeah, she looks devastated. We should probably take away her shoelaces, and that sharp letter opener, too. Just to be safe."

Fine. So she'd been transparent. So both Natalie and David had remarked on Serena closing down the office just so the three of them could eat together. She was more interested in self-preservation than convincing subterfuge, Serena told herself as they drove toward the Caribbean place David had suggested.

With her stomach at full occupancy with knots and butterflies, Serena hadn't cared one way or the other where they went for lunch. Natalie had easily agreed to the restaurant, as well, not that she was likely to be that hungry since she'd been devouring David with her eyes. Actually, Serena thought, fidgeting as Natalie laughed appreciatively at David's tale of lost luggage when he'd come home for Christmas, her assistant seemed to be accelerating through her normal grief process with record-breaking speed. She'd been ogling David with prurient interest since he walked into Inventive Events twenty minutes ago. Not that Serena blamed her—what red-blooded woman with working eyesight wouldn't look at him that way?—but David was *not* a candidate for rebound sex.

And I'm not jealous, I'm feeling protective of a good friend. He would appreciate her looking out for him. Absolutely. Nothing men hated more than being used for recreational no-strings nookie by curvy femme fatales.

"Argh."

"Did you say something?" Natalie called over her shoulder. Once Natalie had found her alligator hair clip in her purse to hold her long hair back, they'd agreed it was too beautiful a day to leave the top up, and the resulting wind was loud enough that Serena could mutter whatever she liked back there without being heard.

So she stuck to denial. "Nope."

In the rearview mirror, David's eyes, sky-blue and seriously amused, met hers. He hadn't stopped grinning since Serena's white lie in the parking lot, when she'd claimed Natalie got queasy if she didn't ride up front. Normally, her friend was more intuitive about backing Serena up. Today, Natalie had looked startled by Serena's announcement, then winked at David. "She must have me confused with someone else. Some of my best memories took place in the back seats of cars."

Serena's muscles had tensed with unwanted possessiveness even as she'd tried to tell herself life would be simpler if Natalie diverted David's attention.

He'd proven difficult to distract, however, and had merely smiled at Natalie's remark. "I know what you mean—there's a couch I feel the same way about." His gaze had flicked to Serena's, and she'd wanted to kiss him. Desperately.

Which, of course, was why it was such a good thing Natalie had agreed to join them.

An hour later, however, Serena was having a difficult time maintaining her goodwill. While Serena sat at the table and contemplated drowning herself in her black bean soup—not that her companions would even notice, much less offer mouth-to-mouth—David and Natalie carried on an animated discussion about fishing. Ick. Serena, vegetarian and soft-hearted wuss, couldn't get too revved about a sport that involved a living creature gasping its last breath as it flopped around in front of her. But Natalie had spent lots of time on her dad's boat, and David had grown up on the coast.

Well, hell. Serena had never needed Patrick as a buffer. She could've just introduced David to Natalie sooner.

Deep down, she knew her crankiness had nothing to do with lures (the kind being discussed *or* the ones Natalie was sending David's way with her hazel eyes). Serena was grouchy because she'd barely slept all weekend, because David would be leaving in the morning, and because her body was tense with repressed sexual need. Typically speaking, she wasn't a big believer in repression.

So why aren't you going for it, nitwit? He was ready, willing and able the other morning.

Hell, she'd been more than ready herself. She'd been hot

and needy, shattering at his touch so quickly it had verged on embarrassing. Just the memory of it made her mouth go dry. He made her feel like no one else ever had, which was ironic, really. Because if he'd *been* anyone else, other than David Grant of the esteemed Savannah Grants, they might have had a chance.

Every year she saw David, he was another rung up the corporate ladder and looking more conservative, though, granted, few men had ever made conservative seem so sexy. He worked long hours and had endless stories about corporate dinners or business travel. They were entertaining, but mostly because she enjoyed laughing at some of the absurdities of that lifestyle. It certainly wasn't one she wanted for herself, even by extension.

Sure, she'd taken business classes—possibly some freak genetic coding she'd inherited—but she'd used the background to start her own company, doing what *she* wanted in order to maintain creative control and not slave for a bunch of suits. She worked hard, but she left the office behind when she went home for the day. Her father had constantly been worried about impressing his superiors, wanting his wife to dress more "appropriately" at a business dinner, spending Saturdays on a yacht with the regional vice president instead of using his visitation rights to see the daughter he'd been quick to dismiss—unless she'd done something he could brag about or the bank was sponsoring a father-daughter event.

Though Serena had a higher opinion of David than to think ever losing custody of a child would come as a relief to him, she also knew how important his family's opinion was to him. How determined he was to prove himself equal to previous Grants. The man came from a family of senators, for crying out loud! Serena, who had been half-heartedly raised by her mother and neighbors who helped look after her during her teenage years so she didn't miss classes during any of Tricia's walkabouts, once filled in as the nude art model for a friend's class. Not exactly the image of the corporate significant other. Considering how James and Meredith viewed her choices, she could just *imagine* how the Grants would look at her.

"Serena?"

The sound of David's voice jolted her from contemplating her cold soup. "Huh?"

"We figured we'd lost you," Natalie said, staring at her boss with a perplexed expression before turning back to David. "See, this is what I mean. She insists she's over him, but anyone can see she's totally preoccupied."

"You do seem unusually pensive." David brushed his fingers over the back of Serena's hand, and so many fizzing embers shot through her she felt like a human sparkler. "Miss Patrick?"

"No." As difficult as it was to meet David's eyes, she had no other choice. It was imperative that he knew no other man had been on her mind when he'd been touching her, kissing her, setting her on fire, bringing her to or— "If you two would excuse me, I'm just not feeling myself. I think I'm gonna splash a little water on my face or something. Maybe I'm getting one of those spring colds."

"That could be it," David said, his completely unconvinced grin making her want to throw a little water in *his* face.

David watched his best friend flee the table, sighing to himself and wondering how long it would take her just to be honest about what she wanted—him. Arrogant, perhaps, but true.

Good thing he was a patient man.

"She's got it bad for you," Natalie mused, startling him with her observation.

He jerked his gaze back toward the smiling brunette, unsure how to handle the situation. He doubted the woman would've been flirting so blatantly if Serena had shared intimate details with her. And if Serena hadn't, then it probably wasn't his place…though he wouldn't mind an ally.

"What makes you say that?" he asked carefully.

Natalie rolled her twinkling eyes. "Oh, please. She's been about as convincing in her *dis*interest as you've been in your interest of me."

He hadn't gone so far as feigning attraction, not wanting to lead Natalie on, but it had occurred to him that a little friendly conversation with the woman might help his cause.

"I've genuinely enjoyed talking to you," he said sheepishly.

"Well, who wouldn't? But I gather you'd enjoy…other things with her more. You've told her how you feel?"

Told her? He'd shown her, in some of the most explicit ways imaginable. For all the good it had done him. He hadn't seen Serena this stubborn since an environmental rights protest in college, when he'd wound up having to bail her out of jail. He'd given her hell about it for days.

Natalie chuckled. "Well, I see now why she never seemed that upset about Patrick's defection. Any woman with half a brain would rather have you."

"Too bad Serena doesn't share that opinion."

"Oh, yes she does. I'm not sure why she isn't acting on it. I have to admit, cute as you are, most of my comments today were just to needle her, to make sure I wasn't misreading her. I've never seen her like this." Natalie picked up the dessert menu, adding, "Normally, if Serena has a thought or emotion, she goes with it."

That would be Tricia's influence, he guessed. Since he and Serena had grown close after she'd moved away from home, he'd never met either of her parents, but over the years he'd pieced together a pretty clear picture. Tricia "Embrace Life" Donavan was the one who threw herself into every undertaking wholeheartedly—sometimes to the exclusion of what was going on around her—whether it was her daughter's art project for school, an angry divorce or a sudden yen to visit the Grand Canyon. He gathered she'd been an exciting mother, but not the most stable guardian. Then there was Serena's father, James, who, until last year, hadn't seemed to have much post-divorce contact with his daughter, except for the instances when he'd taken time to express mild disapproval over something.

There was really no part of Serena's upbringing to which David could relate. His parents might not be given to the same outpourings as Serena's mother, but in their own conservative way, they loved each other and their children. On the occasions Serena had mentioned her parents' divorce, her offhand comments had made David want to knock James's and Tricia's heads together. It sounded as though Tricia had been caught up in her own melodrama, dragging Serena into the bitter divorce with little regard for its effect on her daughter, and James hadn't been able to separate his growing censure for his wife from his child.

David sighed, realizing that Serena's wariness stemmed from far more than their respective financial backgrounds. If he hadn't been so blinded by his own lust, that would have occurred to him sooner. But her parents' past had noth-

ing to do with here and now—a point that would be easier
to make if the woman he was trying to convince would stop
hiding behind other people and in public rest rooms.

6

DAVID DRUMMED his fingers on the base of his keyboard as he reread the light e-mail, with its interest in how his move was progressing and its playful teasing. Serena had indicated he not only needed to find an apartment, he needed to find someone to help him "break it in." He'd heard it was good luck to make love in every room of a new place...but the woman he wanted wasn't volunteering. In fact, in her opening, she'd mentioned Natalie asking after him and wrote, "the two of you really seemed to hit it off."

Even if she was using the e-mail as an excuse to tell him to look elsewhere for sex, at least she was comfortable enough to bring it up. By the time he'd said goodbye to her a week and a half ago before returning to Boston, she'd been uncharacteristically quiet and had barely met his gaze.

When he'd first learned he was moving to Atlanta, David had been confident he could win Serena over. But that only worked if she was around to be won. *She's not going to provide you the opportunity.* Given the way she'd been "too busy" to see him at Christmas and how she'd gradually withdrawn from him over the weekend—bringing Natalie to that last lunch and only at ease again when he was eight states away—he realized that just being in the same city didn't necessarily give him the chance he needed.

What he really needed was a strategy for thwarting her avoidance.

A knock sounded against the doorjamb, and David minimized his e-mail as he glanced up at Lou Innes. Wearing a polo shirt, casual slacks and an embroidered golf visor, Lou obviously planned to take advantage of the warm weather this week and hit the greens.

"What can I do for you?" David asked.

"Just dropped by to see how things were going. Your last week with us here in Beantown, huh?"

David nodded. His place was packed and ready for the movers, and his parents had been thrilled when he'd called a couple of nights ago to announce the move. "I'm ready to get the new office up and running and take Atlanta by storm."

"Good, good. You've seemed rather…intense since your return. We wanted to make sure we weren't putting too much on you with this transfer. You've got quite a future with this company, and we don't want you burning out on us." The words were of the just-looking-out-for-you variety, but behind his wire-rimmed glasses, Lou's eyes were calculating.

Damn. Was Lou having doubts about the decision? "Oh, no. No burnout here. I've just been concentrating on everything I can do for AGI with this relocation." In the following weeks, David just needed to make sure his determination was clear to Lou all the way from Georgia.

"Glad to hear it. The job will be demanding, especially the first few months. We want to make our presence in Atlanta known quickly and effectively." Lou grinned. "But maybe in a few years, *you'll* be able to take the afternoon off for business golf and leave the company in some capable up-and-comer's hands."

David laughed. "That's all right, I don't have a decent swing anyway. What I do have are appointments for lunch next week with several important businessmen in Atlanta and ideas for civic projects that will help announce our arrival to the community in a positive light."

"Well, then." Lou looked pleased with the information. "You just forget I even dropped by and carry on with your work."

Easier said than done, David admitted to himself once he was alone again.

In the past, he'd always enjoyed the demanding challenges of his job. Maybe at some point, his efforts had been about male pride or proving he wasn't like some of his more odious relatives, content to live on trust funds or cushy jobs they'd been given because of who they were, but David had genuinely become a dedicated executive determined to reach the top. Yet after all the work he'd done to reach this point, not even his excitement for heading up the corporate relocation was enough to distract him from Serena for long.

Get your head back in the game, man. Too bad there wasn't a way to combine his two biggest passions—his job and Serena. Unless… He sat back in his leather chair suddenly, knowing there must be an invisible light bulb over his head right now. Maybe there *was* a way to combine the two.

A WEEK. Serena paused while jotting notes on her day planner Monday morning, realizing that David had now been in Atlanta for an entire week. And she'd yet to see him.

Oh, he'd called to tell her about the corporate hotel efficiency suite he was staying in while he continued to search for a permanent place. He'd asked her if business had picked up, groused about traffic and told her to tell Natalie hello. He'd let her vent about the strained phone call from her future stepmother and Meredith's apologetic explanation that with both of her children doing readings at the wedding, as well as James's brother, they'd decided four would be overkill and had changed their minds about Serena doing one. But talking aside, David hadn't visited her or even mentioned their seeing each other in the near future.

Serena honestly couldn't tell if she was disappointed or relieved.

What did you think was going to happen?

She'd made her feelings to him clear, and he was respecting them. Plus, he was swamped right now. She only ran an office for two and had encountered the occasional snafu with things like computer lines being installed or the right phone number not working. David was responsible for hiring new Atlanta personnel and getting the office ready for the few dozen employees that would be transferred from the four AGI locations around the country. He'd admitted to possibly losing an apartment to someone else because he'd missed his appointed walk-through in favor of meeting with the CEO of some cell-phone conglomerate to discuss how AGI technology could improve cellular communications. If not even finding a place to live was a priority, he certainly didn't have time for Serena.

The thought gave her a twinge of painful déjà vu, and she blinked. She wasn't a kid anymore, wishing someone would pay her more attention. She was self-sufficient and had plenty of her own concerns to keep her busy, such as the promotional efforts she'd been coordinating to grow her company and the surprise party she was supposed to be planning for Alyson's twenty-seventh birthday. So why the restless annoyance and confusion because David had given up?

Not that she wanted him to try to change her mind—no, the safe distance was much, um, safer—but she didn't think she'd ever seen him concede defeat so easily. Come to think of it, she'd never seen him concede defeat. Then again, why would a man who could have his choice of women much better suited to him continue pursuing one who claimed not to want him?

Claimed being the key word. Because just the sound of his voice on the other end of the phone was enough to spark tremors inside her.

Funny, when Meredith had once proposed introducing Serena to some "nice young businessmen," James had interrupted with a disappointed, "I think you'll find the young men we know aren't Serena's type."

That was probably true, although she wondered just exactly what her father deemed her "type." He'd be stunned to learn David Grant, consummate businessman and grandson of a congressman, was the one who dominated her thoughts. Thoughts, fantasies...

Could she really turn David away if he suggested their going to bed again? Her eager body quivered at the thought of making love to him. *No, no, no. You are not going to sleep with him.* If she was smart, she wouldn't even get within twenty feet of him. So it was good that he was too busy at work for them to see each other. Besides, she had her own job to do.

"Hey, boss?" Natalie's voice came through the speaker-intercom on Serena's phone.

Serena sighed, grateful for the interruption. "Yes?"

"You have time for an appointment at ten-thirty?"

"Depends on whether or not it would take longer than about twenty minutes." Serena glanced at her day planner. "I should get out of here by eleven if I'm going to get to that caterer's on time."

The intercom line went dead, as Natalie presumably returned to her phone call and relayed news of Serena's schedule. Serena exhaled, thinking that a meeting with a new client would be a very good thing.

She'd recently sunk a large chunk of change into advertising, knowing that in business you had to spend money to make it, but now she was waiting nervously to see if the investment would pay off. She couldn't afford to be thinking about David instead of her customers and what she could do to make each of their events memorable and flawless. With that reminder, she got back to work, making calls to a local deejay, a small airport—for a couple who wanted a sky-diving wedding—and a hotel with an outdoor patio she'd reserved for a client's "Midsummer's Night" bash.

Ten-thirty arrived before she knew it, and she was just pulling out her compact and some lip-gloss when someone knocked on her door. Natalie. The receptionist wasn't at her desk and hadn't announced anyone's arrival. Surely she wouldn't have ducked out when they were expecting a client.

"Come on in," Serena called, pursing her lips in front of the small handheld mirror.

"Hope you're not applying makeup for my benefit."

At the sound of David's voice, she jumped. Her tube of Really Rum Raisin rolled beneath the desk.

"Because I've always thought you looked just as beautiful without it," he added as he walked toward her.

"Hey. Y-you startled me." But her accelerated pulse had as much to do with the way his pale-blue shirt made his eyes glow as it did with her surprise at seeing him.

He bent down for a moment, then straightened. "I believe this is yours?"

"Thanks." Serena reached out to take the gloss, trying not to brush his fingers with her own but failing. Waves of warmth coursed through her, and she was grateful for the piece of furniture separating their bodies. "I'm glad you dropped by, but I'm afraid I have an app—"

"I'm the appointment, Serena. Meet your ten-thirty."

Serena narrowed her eyes. Natalie was a dead woman. "By any chance, did you pass my receptionist on your way in?"

He nodded, taking a seat in one of the visitor's chairs. "She said she was running down the hall to fill the coffee-pot with water."

Serena sat, too, wishing she was depressed over the lost business instead of so happy to see him. "She led me to believe I'd be meeting with a new client."

"You are." He grinned. "I have a proposition for you."

"I'll just bet." What was the man up to now?

"A *business* proposition. On behalf of AGI, I'd like to hire you for a large charity fund-raiser three weeks from this Saturday."

Three weeks? Was he insane?

He gave her a moment to let his offer sink in, but the pause only confused her, allowing time for conflicting thoughts and emotions. How often had she thrown business Craig's way, buying an extra painting to help fund his groceries—primarily canned soups and produce on sale because the sell-by date was approaching? Was that what

David was doing, friendly charity? She'd told him profit had been low recently, which sounded better than nonexistent. She was partly relieved, partly flattered by his offer. Still...

"This is, um, unexpected. It's nice of you to consider Inventive Events, of course, but—"

"It's not a personal decision. A lot of the bigger services would have required my booking them months ago, or, if they squeezed us in, they wouldn't have the time I'd like devoted to this. I was hoping, if things have been slow for you, that you'd fit us in. I know that's a hefty favor to ask, but a job this size could get the word out about your company. And I know I can work with you, which is important, because I intend to be very hands-on."

Her undisciplined gaze fluttered down to his fingers, and she easily recalled the way they'd played over her skin, the way he'd known exactly when to touch her softly, teasing, and when to be more forceful. *Business, Serena. Focus.*

Her mind was too blank to add anything professional, so he continued his pitch.

"I have a lot on my plate right now, and one of the things AGI wants is for me to announce our presence with a splash and network within the business community. A coalition of local technology companies has been sponsoring an annual fund-raiser to fight breast cancer, with all of them contributing cash but one group acting as the 'host.' They rotate the bulk of responsibilities, but this year's scheduled host company sank its money into a huge software project that flopped. They're pretty busy just trying to avoid bankruptcy and only recently bothered to let the partner sponsors know the ball had been dropped. No one else was excited about trying to take it on last-minute, but the timing of the event is exactly the networking opportunity I want for AGI, if I can put together something smashing in time."

David spoke with a rapid, almost breathless enthusiasm, and she could see how much this opportunity meant to him, how determined he was to make the most of it.

Then he grinned at her, his expression becoming more personal. "Naturally, when I thought 'smashing,' I thought of you."

She laughed at the unnecessary compliment. "Isn't the flattery-will-get-you-everywhere approach a bit clichéd?"

"I prefer to think of it as tried and true."

"My dad's wedding is the weekend before," she hedged, wondering what her stress threshold was for early June. "This really isn't great timing."

"I know. But it won't be for anyone else I try to get last-minute, either. And this will help you out. In return, you get to help me wow Atlanta and raise money for a good cause. So how 'bout it? Say you'll do this, Serena."

She pressed her fingers to her temples, knowing she'd be nine kinds of idiot to turn down the potential word-of-mouth, which would do more than any advertising she bought. "Don't your bosses need to see some kind of proposal first, my ideas or estimated costs?"

"Normally, yes. But there's barely time as it is."

True. "What kind of event did you have in mind?"

"A dinner. The theme is Time to Find a Cure."

Her heart sank. Certainly the cause was a worthy one, but her forte wasn't exactly black-tie charity banquets where people paid three hundred a plate for chicken kiev in a hotel ballroom and schmoozed for a few hours. He was offering her a unique chance to spread the word about her company, but if she was going to build a reputation, she wanted it to be an accurate one. "David, I know this is important to you, and I want to help. But I specialize in events a little different from the norm."

He frowned. "How different did you have in mind?"

She bit her lip. "I'm not sure yet. But if you wanted to go the traditional route, an arts-and-antiques auction or—"

"Serena, I don't want traditional. I want you."

Her gaze flew to his, and her heart pounded at the warm assurance in his voice. The lust she'd been fighting reflected back at her from his eyes. But there was more than just desire there. There was understanding. Affection. Acceptance.

The giddy rush it gave her was so potent her eyes actually welled with tears she rapidly blinked away.

"Obviously I have to be able to sell everyone on it," he added quickly, "but I want it to have your personal touch. To be fun."

"All right," she agreed. "I'll do you."

His eyebrows shot up.

"Do this job for you, I meant." Brilliant. Just the Freudian slip she'd needed to keep things professional and platonic.

"It doesn't have to be an either-or situation," he said with a broad grin. "I'd be happy to let you do both."

She cleared her throat. "You know what, an auction might be good, now that I think about it. I'm picturing…men." Actually, she'd been picturing him. Naked. But she tried to use that to springboard to something more productive.

His wary expression reminded her of someone who'd stepped off the high-dive and had only just noticed the drop. "Men? I'm not sure where you're going with this."

"A bachelor auction!" Why not? That wasn't even far out in left field. "A gladiator, a cowboy, a firefighter—"

"I'm picturing the Village People," he interrupted, his scowl having gone past caution straight to discreet panic.

She glared. Sure, he *said* he trusted her, but he'd have a completely different tone of voice right now if she'd just suggested the chicken kiev and a silent art auction. Disappointment cramped her belly, and the skeptical expression in his eyes reminded her unpleasantly of her father. And that one well-meaning business professor who'd kept insisting she had the brains to succeed if she'd just change her approach.

But this is David. He knows you, and he asked *for your personal touch.* If he was serious about giving her a chance, then she owed him the same.

She took a deep breath, exhaling away the negativity and the initial excitement that had kept her from articulating the idea better. "You said the theme is Time to Find a Cure, right? And there are a coalition of companies that will be listed as sponsors? Then we should have a decent pool of eligible men to use from the different businesses. The evening's host—you?—can start with a prepared statement about all of the things mankind has managed to do since time began. The invention of fire, going to the moon. And, soon, we hope, with the generous donations of people like yourselves, a cure for cancer."

David crossed his arms. "Not bad so far. Go on."

"Admission will be one way to raise money, but after the dinner, we'll auction off dates for charity. Each bachelor can be in costume, representing a different period. Vikings, knights, swashbucklers, cowboys…all the basic female fantasies."

"Hmm. Might take some cajoling, but in the end, I think most of the guys will be won over by the chance to be a woman's living fantasy." His blue eyes took on a speculative gleam as he sat forward. "So, what's yours? Fantasy, I mean."

"I, uh…" She tried to come up with something that was David's total opposite, something that would thwart his advances, discourage him from coming around the desk, leaning her back in her chair and laying siege to her willpower with hot breathless kisses. Right. Because that would be bad. "Bikers. Yeah, that's it. Leather-clad bad boys."

His eyes widened, then he laughed. "So you're a Hell's Angels kind of gal?"

"All the way." Sheesh. "Can't resist a guy with a pig."

"It's possible the word you were looking for there was *hog*."

"That's not what I said?" She glanced pointedly at the day planner on her desk. "Did I mention I have to be going soon?"

"Natalie warned me when I set up the appointment." He sighed, then resumed his no-nonsense demeanor. "Actually, you gave me an idea with the motorcycles. Maybe we should auction off something macho and high-dollar. Let's assume that most of the men attending won't be bidding on the bachelors."

Serena nodded thoughtfully. "We could have an ongoing silent auction throughout the evening, where prospective buyers, men and women, could write down bids on props."

"What kind of props?"

"Something that corresponds loosely to each of our themed bachelors. A collector's edition pistol for the cowboy, state-of-the-art fishing equipment for a buccaneer. I did say loosely. This is all off the top of my head."

He laughed. "No, I like it. Let me present this to the investors. Damn, I wish we had more time. The good news is, the venue's already booked, so we don't have to worry about where we're going to have this thing. But the details are all up in the air, thanks to the jokers who let it slide. I'm doing final interviews tomorrow morning for my receptionist, but how about I pick you up for lunch? That gives us both tonight to jot down thoughts and you time to outline what might need to be done."

Good to be back on steady, impersonal ground. "It would have to be a late lunch, but that sounds perfect. Let's nail down specifics as soon as possible, and I'll take it from there."

"*We'll* take it from there," he corrected. "Don't worry, I have no intention of getting in your way, but I do plan to be very closely involved in the decisions on everything. I'm being entrusted with funds from a number of people, and after the way this was disastrously mismanaged the first time, I want to be able to report back to everyone with concrete explanations of what's being done."

He flashed her a wolfish grin. "So you and I will be spending a great deal of time together."

7

"*THIS IS* your idea of a business lunch?" Serena stood in the parking lot with her hands on her hips.

Her first surprise had been when David walked into her office in a green polo shirt and jeans, unusually casual for a Tuesday afternoon meeting. Then he'd ushered her out to his newly leased convertible—he'd really liked the model he'd rented on his last trip—and showed her the basket of chips, sandwiches and fresh fruit.

"A picnic," she said incredulously. Not that spending the afternoon rolling around on a blanket with this man didn't sound appealing. "I thought this was strictly professional."

He pressed a hand to his heart, his eyes wide in unconvincing fake surprise. "I can't believe you of all people are so incapable of thinking outside the box. I just moved back down South and would like to take advantage of the gorgeous environment. Is there any reason we can't talk about dinner arrangements and sound systems while eating outside?"

"No."

But she wasn't buying his act, either. He reached past her, brushing her body just slightly, to open her car door. Somehow, he seemed like a man with more than just sound systems on his mind.

"I can't shake the feeling I've been had," she muttered.

He chuckled as he pushed the door closed. "Honey, if you'd been had, you'd know it."

Her suspicions about the afternoon outing were heightened when he drove them to a park. They passed a parked truck and a jogger, but with kids still in school and the forecast calling for rain later, the grounds were fairly deserted. They followed a winding road around a man-made lake and up a little ridge that led to the back of the park, and David stopped beneath some trees that overlooked the water. In a couple of weeks, the area would be packed with swimmers and people wanting to take out their boats, but today it was breezy and subdued.

"Secluded spot you picked," she observed as David unrolled a thick fleecy blanket under some trees.

"I thought the shade would be nice," he countered.

"Convenient." Never mind the fact that the sun kept disappearing behind clouds.

He plopped down between the basket and the small well-stocked cooler he'd brought along. "I don't know about you, but I'm starving."

His intentions aside, the veggie sub on whole wheat he'd brought her would definitely hit the spot. She kicked off her shoes and placed them on the corners of the blanket, which kept rustling in the wind. Despite her misgivings, he really did want to discuss business. She'd spent yesterday evening putting together a summary of her ideas and everything that needed to be done, and he leafed through all of them, asking rapid-fire questions and sharing his own suggestions.

In seemingly no time, she'd devoured her sandwich, followed by a bag of chips, and they'd filled three pages of notes. David finished off the contents of a container of fresh fruit and packed the trash into the basket, away from the steadily increasing breeze. Then he stretched out on the blanket, lying on his side with his weight supported on his elbow. When she asked for a tentative head count of auctionees, he rattled off names of eligible bachelors in his office.

Serena, sitting near his feet with her legs bent to the side, flicked his calf with her pen. "What about you? You've conveniently left yourself off this list," she teased.

"I don't have to go on the block. As you pointed out, I'll be the evening's emcee."

Secretly, she was thrilled he wouldn't be standing in front of a roomful of women who suited his life better than she did, offering a romantic outing to the highest bidder. But that didn't mean she couldn't needle him about it. "You want to set the precedent for the other companies, don't you? Gain acclaim for AGI?"

He sat up, his gaze suddenly intrigued, predatory, like a wild animal who had just spotted something fun to toy with. "Would you bid on me, Serena?"

A flush warmed not only her face but her entire body. Her very sensitive, very aware body. "No. This is for charity, remember? We want people to fork over the big bucks, and, um, my bucks are pretty small." She was glad people were willing to shell out the money to help with this incredibly worthwhile cause, but she was reminded yet again that David and the people he knew operated in a different reality than hers.

"Small can be good." His gaze strayed to her chest, and her nipples tightened in anticipation.

She fidgeted, hoping her dark orange top masked her aroused response. It was ridiculous to be so turned on when all the man had done was look at her. "I think for moneymaking purposes, small is bad. Moving on... The guys may need some help coming up with romantic outings. It should be appealing, but not uncomfortably intimate for the bachelor and the winner. And we want to be careful to offer a variety of prize packages. Not every girl wants a candlelight dinner, necessarily. One couple could have box seats at a Braves game, another—"

"What would *you* want?"

She focused on the legal pad she held, as if he'd asked a life-or-death question whose answer could only be found on the sheet of paper in her hands. "Since we've already covered the fact that I don't have the money to bid, I don't think—"

"Just for brainstorming purposes." He scooted closer on the soft green blanket, and she breathed in the scent of his soap, the warmth of his skin. "If you did buy me and make me yours for the evening...what would you do with me?"

She laughed nervously. "Be more careful when you talk to other people about the auction, so our bachelors don't sound like gigolos. You want to make the front page because we raised a lot of money for a good cause, not because vice shut us down."

"You seem to be having trouble with the brainstorming concept. Let me help kick-start your creativity," he offered in a sexy drawl. "Say you were the one up for auction. Want me to tell you what *I'd* do with *you*?"

"No!" Couldn't he demonstrate instead, her evil libido asked. *Double no.* "I think we're getting off track."

"Not at all. You brought up a good point. Sure, most of the bids are going to be charity-driven, but there's no reason we can't offer evenings women actually enjoy. So it's my job to figure out what women want."

"If ever there was a man up to that task," she muttered, too lost in his eyes to censor her words.

"Oh, trust me, honey." His hands curved around her shoulders. "I am very much up for it."

Her breathing had turned shallow and ragged. "How do you do this?"

She had to ask. Here she was struggling to concentrate on what might be the biggest job of her career thus far, and he switched back and forth from sex to business with no problem. Besides, continuing not to address what was going on between them was as ludicrous as pretending not to see a six-ton elephant. "How do you shut it off and turn it on so smoothly? How can you be talking about budget constraints one minute, all blasé and relaxed, and effortlessly seducing me the next?"

His smile was wry. "I don't exactly shut it off, but I've had practice dealing with it…those all-night study sessions we did before finals?"

She swallowed. He'd been attracted to her in college? As they'd gotten to know each other, dropping personal tidbits here and there between academic discussions, they'd flirted some, but it was mostly of the obnoxious variety, ragging on each other's dates and bantering, not "I must have you."

"You wanted me then?" Her voice came out in a disbelieving whisper.

"I can't remember when I didn't want you."

The wind caught a few strands of her hair, and David brushed them back, resting his hand on her cheek. "And if you think I'm relaxed, well…"

He glanced downward, pointedly, and she followed with her own gaze. *Hello.* Even the thickness of the denim couldn't hide the erection straining against his zipper.

Heat swept through her, obliterating her defenses. That someone like David could be so turned on by her…not just now, but apparently for the entire time he'd known her? For so much of her life, she'd felt as if she was struggling with the people she loved, to no avail. Trying to get her father's approval, trying to get her mother's attention.

Then there was David, always there when she needed him, knowing how to make her laugh, how to make her body sing. When he lowered his head to kiss her, she could no more have pushed him away than she could have condoned censorship of the arts. Hell, she barely knew how she'd managed to resist him *this* long.

His hands cupped her head, and she kissed him gently at first, tracing his lips, smiling at the way he tasted salty from the potato chips and sweet from the strawberries. Then he slid his tongue into her mouth, and she forgot about gentleness as he stabbed it in and out in rhythmic, suggestive thrusts that replaced rational thought with sensual frenzy. She gripped his shoulders, meeting his ardor with her own, too-long denied.

It was in a desire-blurred haze that she registered him laying her back on the soft blanket, pressing his weight against her. Her legs, bare beneath the hem of her skirt, tangled with his, the rough caress of the denim on her skin heightening her awareness as he shifted, bringing his erection into tantalizing contact with where her body burned the most.

He balanced himself above her, his tone raw with passion. "Other women don't affect me like this. Just you. And I don't believe other men make you feel this way."

Definitely not. She stared into his eyes—far bluer than the sky today—but couldn't bring herself to admit the truth in what he'd said, unsure what the confession would cost her later.

But he wasn't content merely to accept her consenting silence. "Do they?"

He lifted one of her hands to his lips, dropped a kiss against it, then explored each finger with his mouth, tasting, sucking, nipping with his teeth just enough for a little squeak to catch in her throat. Then he surprised her by turning her hand around and pressing it against her breast, which ached for attention, the pebbled peak thrusting forward.

"Do you get this turned on for anyone else, Serena? This wet?"

It was a guess on his part, but an accurate one. She *was* wet—drenched, practically dripping. Her skin felt tingly and tight, inadequate for holding in the restless fire that shot through her whenever David touched her body.

He brushed her own hand back and forth over her nipple. The fabric of her shirt and silky tease of her bra did nothing to diminish the sensation. Each stroke sent little arrows of need to her abdomen. He let go of her, skimming his hand past her stomach. Her insides fluttered, and she experienced a shiver of anticipation, knowing where he was going but not how long he'd make her wait before he got there.

Reaching below the hem of her short skirt, he ran his fingers along the damp feminine cleft shielded by her panties. He tugged her underwear down legs that trembled with the same exertion as if she'd run a marathon, then his touch returned, tracing a teasing path over the narrow strip of hair that covered her.

He clasped her hand again, guiding her. "Feel what we do to each other."

It was an erotic, surreal sensation, her hand moving beneath his direction, as though she were experiencing herself through his senses, feeling what he must when he touched her. The slippery liquid heat, the swollen bud of her clit, the velvety folds of flesh that would envelop him when he slid inside her. Moaning, she thrashed underneath him, desperate for him to be inside her. Her fingers continued to move reflexively when he let go of her.

But then she realized she could be touching *him*.

She rolled to her side, grappling with his shirt and wanting it over his head and out of the way so she could kiss him again. Once she'd accomplished that, she raked her fingers across his chest, hearing her own muffled cry when he captured her mouth, sucking on her tongue. Somewhere during the kiss, they shifted positions so that he was on his back and she was draped sideways over him, kissing the corded muscle along his neck all the way down his shoulder to one flat brown male nipple. The caress inspired him to raise his hand beneath her shirt, shoving down one satiny cup of her bra until her breast popped out.

He strummed his fingers over her, brushing the now exposed sensitive underside, trailing upward in wide circles that ringed the aching, taut peak. Continuing that, he lifted his head and lightly bit the other nipple through her shirt. Serena gasped, her arousal so fierce it was a pang inside her.

She blindly sought his zipper, and the quiet metal rasp beneath the overlaying sound of the distant birds on the breeze was sweet music to her ears. He was rock-hard, and she moved aside the smooth cotton of his briefs, freeing him to her touch. She circled him with her fist, squeezing with gentle, insistent pressure, watching his face and the intense desire etched in his tight expression. Closing his eyes, he swore, then whispered her name, falling back and letting her set the pace between them.

Good thing.

If he thought now was one of those times to subject her to a slow, sensual exploration, he was insane. Her body had hungered for his for months. A bout of his teasing, leisurely lovemaking would probably kill her right now. Besides, just because they hadn't run into anyone—and were less likely to as the afternoon turned cooler and cloudier—didn't mean it would be smart to prolong this. She tightened her grip, sliding her fingers along his shaft, rubbing her thumb across the slick, engorged head, her heart accelerating with the sheer joy of finally having him.

She struggled to catch her breath. "Y-you have a condom?"

He yanked his jeans down, taking his briefs at the same time, then pulled a wallet out of his back pocket. His hands actually shook as he sheathed himself. Knees bent at her sides, she straddled his thighs, the crisp hair on his legs brushing her delicate skin, his body firm and scorchingly hot to the touch. Her skirt swept over him in a gentle *swish swish* like the lapping of waves, a quiet counterpoint to her pounding pulse and their frenzied breathing.

David let loose another expletive, running his hand over the clothes she still wore. "I waited all this time, and I'm not going to get to see you?"

"Guess you'll just have to use..." She sank down by painfully slow degrees, feeling herself expand around the tip of him, stretching deliciously. "Your. Imagin—*oh*."

He was fully inside her, filling her in a way that was so damn good it was almost unbearable. David clasped her hips beneath her skirt, his fingers digging into her skin in wordless encouragement. She rocked her weight back, lifting herself off him, almost experimentally, before sliding back down, her body memorizing the feel of him and luxuriating in making love again. But the urges she'd been resisting so long overcame her, greedy in their demands and causing her to undulate against him.

As she settled into a vigorous rhythm, he raked one hand over the neckline of her shirt, dragging it downward until her breasts peeked over the top, giving him free access. The cool air, damp with the promise of coming rain, chilled her skin, and her already distended nipples puckered further, wickedly lifted and framed by the repositioned clothing.

She paused, clenching her muscles around him, and flashed a brief smile. "Happy now?"

"Almost." His eyes locked with hers, and he reached beneath the pooled fabric of her skirt to trail along her thighs toward her center. He pressed his thumb against her, doubling her stimulation as he caressed her and thrust inside her at the same time, and she rode him with increased urgency.

He cupped his other palm around the curve of her butt, flexing his hips up to meet her, surging deeper into her. "I want to touch you everywhere at once."

"Maybe I can help." She felt decadently exposed, lushly displayed for him in the most powerful, feminine way. Her fingers danced across her chest, plucking at a rigid nipple, then the other. Piercing arousal darted through her body, from erogenous zone to zone.

She closed her eyes, caught in the maelstrom, all the surrounding sounds of nature drowned out by the soft slap of her body meeting his. He kept pace with her, moving inside her and working his fingers in a wicked circle, knowing just how to keep her teetering desperately on the brink—timeless, weightless, lost to everything but the immediate physical sensations wracking her body.

But not even David with all his sensual finesse could keep her suspended there forever. Her climax burst through in a blinding flash, her body erupting in spasms of relief and pleasure. She collapsed against his chest, murmuring his name as he pumped into her for the last few thrusts before finding his own release.

With one hand splayed against the small of her back, he trailed his fingers up and down her spine, caressing her in the sudden stillness after so much frenetic motion. Serena's mind felt fragmented, and she wondered if she'd ever get all the pieces put back together in a cohesive whole.

Maybe it was best if she didn't. She'd rather not think about what they'd done. She wanted to just lie here and—

Ka-*boom*.

The clap of thunder shook the ground beneath them, and rain began pelting down. If it was meant to be divine interruption, it was apparently on time-delay. With the shelter of tree branches above them filtering the rain, Serena wasn't soaked yet, but it would only be a matter of time. She scurried to her feet, scooping her discarded undies off the blanket.

David was quick to follow, taking on the more difficult task of trying to slide on damp denim. She packed their things into the car as he struggled with his jeans, then joined her. He put the key in the ignition and quickly put the top up.

"Not the ending to our lunch I was hoping for," he told her, running his hand through his damp hair and scattering a few droplets. "But I am fast associating you with forces of nature."

His grin brought to mind that first tumultuous time they'd made love, a night she had told him later was a mistake. Satisfying, earth-shattering and incomparable, but a mistake all the same. And what had changed since then? He was still David Grant, of the Savannah Grants, on the fast track to yuppie success, and she was still...

"David."

She didn't have to look in his direction to tell that his entire body tensed.

"Don't," he ordered softly. "I hope to God I'm wrong, but you have that this-was-a-slipup-and-should-never-happen-again note in your voice."

"There's a good reason for that."

He smacked his palm against the steering wheel. "Dammit, Serena."

"I—"

"Not right now. Not yet." He scowled darkly at her. "Maybe no one's ever told you this, but it's a breach of etiquette to tell a man you just want to be friends five minutes after you've made him come."

THE RIDE back to Serena's office was tense, and even though David himself had been the one to delay the conversation, the gloomy silence was rubbing his nerves raw. The only words she'd spoken had been when she called Natalie from his cell phone and asked her to lock up the office, as Serena wouldn't be back in today. David hadn't said anything, either, because he barely trusted himself to carry on a civil dialogue until after he'd calmed down.

How could she do this to him? Again!

He'd connected with her back there, he knew he had. And not just in the obvious physical way. He'd seen that moment in her eyes, when he'd really reached her, when she'd understood his feelings for her and felt the same for him. But now she was refuting all that?

That could make working with her over the next couple of weeks awkward.

The rain had subsided to a grim sprinkle by the time he parked his car next to hers, but the overcast sky had turned the early evening unusually dark.

She reached for her seat belt, sighing heavily. "This can't keep happening."

"I couldn't agree more." With the taste of her kisses still on his lips and the scent of her body on his, he wanted her more than ever. But they couldn't stay stuck in this frustrating-as-hell pattern of hers.

Her eyebrows shot up as if she'd expected an argument. "Then you won't try to change my mind?"

"I didn't say that." He still thought he was right about them, that if she would get past some superficial differences, she'd realize how much they had in common. Like the explosive chemistry that rendered the rest of the world nonexistent, for starters.

"David." Her voice held a note of warning. "You've hired me to do a job for you, one that's important to both of us. I need you to respect my professional boundaries."

Needed him to respect her escape clause, she meant. "How would you define those boundaries?"

"Well, no sex goes without saying."

He couldn't help noticing she said it anyway. When was she going to be honest with herself about what she really wanted? As her friend, the least he could do was help her face it.

"Deal," he said slowly. "I won't have sex with you. I won't even bring sex up. I won't try to kiss you."

She looked startled by this. "Really?"

"Really." He paused a moment before adding his condition. "Unless, of course, *you* initiate any of that. And aren't going to bolt afterward."

Her jaw tightened. "Boy are you in for a long wait."

"Not exactly." He knew his next words would probably sound autocratic, but if it came out as an obnoxious ultimatum, well…she couldn't be the only one calling the shots between them. He'd never felt quite this way about another woman, but if there was no chance she would let herself return the feeling, he owed it to himself to move the hell on at some point. "I'm waiting three weeks—until the night of the auction. That's it. If we haven't made love by then, it won't happen again."

Her eyes widened at this announcement, but then she scowled. "It won't happen again anyway."

"Call me an optimist. I'm giving you time to consider it." And himself three weeks to do everything in his power to seduce her into admitting what was between them. His promise not to mention sex *directly* didn't prohibit him from saying and doing whatever he could to make her think about it. All was fair in love and war, right?

Because he was beginning to believe that this madness Serena stirred in him could only be love. He'd enjoyed a lot of women, but none had ever caused this fixation. Or extreme annoyance. He'd definitely never been preoccupied with a woman on the job before. With everyone else, he'd been able to do exactly as Serena had said earlier—

shut if off during business hours, during which time he was used to focusing one-hundred percent and working as hard as he could to prove himself.

Serena was like a splinter under his skin, always there. At first, he'd been irritated with his inability to push thoughts of her away and had even begun dating more in Boston, leaving the office earlier than normal to meet a woman for dinner. But nothing had worked and now he had to admit, he enjoyed thinking about Serena. It was the next best thing to being with her.

No other woman inspired him to take time out of his schedule to stop and smell the roses…or make love in the park. When he'd finally quit trying to fight her spell, he'd even found he did his job better. She stimulated him—creatively, intellectually, sexually. They'd come up with some great ideas for the fund-raiser, and he was confident they'd be a good team in all areas.

Now, if only *she'd* stop fighting it.

Which wouldn't happen anytime soon, by the looks of it. Serena opened her door, her expression mutinous in the dim illumination of the car's interior light. "I don't need three weeks, David. I can tell you now my answer is no."

He forced a smile. "I guess we'll see."

"I MEAN, can you even *believe* him?" Serena demanded as she angrily paced her living room.

"Um…no?" Alyson offered from where she sat, wide-eyed, with her knees tucked up against her on the couch.

That damn couch. Serena should've replaced the purple monstrosity months ago!

As soon as she'd arrived home, Serena had called her friend over for a session of meditative yoga. But when

Alyson had arrived, asking what had happened to throw Serena so off balance, everything had bubbled to the surface. Remnants of desire, shards of fear and a truckload of being ticked. Somehow, Serena doubted that focused breathing and the Tree Pose would be enough to restore her calm.

Pacing hadn't done anything to soothe her, either. She dropped into the minifuton chair with a sigh. She realized she held some blame in the situation—she'd ignored caution in favor of indulging her primal desires, and David had been the one to suffer her regret. He had every right to be unhappy with her yo-yo impression, but sheesh... he'd actually threatened her!

"Have sex with me in the next three weeks," she mimicked sarcastically, "or lose conjugal rights forever. I don't even *want* those rights. He's not getting the point!"

Aly tilted her head to the side, toying with the thick rope of auburn hair that fell over her shoulder. "I think *conjugal* only applies to married people."

Serena raised an eyebrow. "Also missing the point."

"Sorry." Her friend smiled. "Just thought it would be fun to set you off again. Are you feeling any better after getting all that out?"

"No." That was the absolute worst part. She felt awful. Not at all relaxed and in harmony with herself, the way one would expect to feel after sex that had affected every muscle in her body and touched her very soul.

Alyson shrugged. "I know you're upset, and I'm not saying he handled the situation with sensitivity, but he's a man. We have to make allowances. Bear in mind that however graceless his words, you're actually getting your way. He's backing off, isn't he? Keeping his hands to himself?"

"You're not going to spoil my righteous outrage by making sense, are you? Maybe I should have called Craig for sympathy instead."

"Are you kidding?" Alyson laughed. "He'd be of no use to you. He and his girlfriend are still in that nauseating deliriously happy phase."

Serena bit her lip. "I haven't met her yet." Actually, she hadn't even realized the woman Craig had mentioned asking out had progressed to girlfriend status. Bad sign— she'd been so preoccupied with David that she'd ignored her friends.

"Well, it's hard to arrange an introduction when the two of them barely come up for air," Alyson said. "But you'll meet her at my birthday party Saturday."

Damn, Serena had practically forgotten Aly's surprise party, as well. "Yeah, I…wait a minute! I—I don't know what you're talking about. Saturday? Your birthday's not even until next week."

"You people are sad," Alyson chided with a shake of her head. "But at least you're more convincing than Craig and that convoluted story he tried to feed me to keep me from making alternate plans this weekend."

"He was supposed to tell you he had a showing he'd love for you to attend!" How difficult could that be?

"He did, but I got so excited for him that he started backpedaling so I wouldn't be disappointed when I found out the truth. Don't worry, I'll practice feigning shock beforehand."

"Thank you." Serena said. What kind of events coordinator was she, anyway, unable to pull off one simple surprise party in a gallery an acquaintance of Craig's was letting them rent for the evening?

Alyson sat forward, propping her chin on her fists. "I suppose you won't be bringing David?"

"Did you hear *anything* I said tonight?"

"Yeah, but I've always wanted to meet him. Besides, I thought your whole rationale for not having sex with him was that you didn't want to spoil the friendship. Friends do stuff like go to the same parties. It would be a smart move on your part to invite him, show him you enjoy his company but are immune to his charms."

"There you go making sense again." A sound plan, really...or it would've been, if Serena had a chance in hell at immunity.

8

WHEN SERENA finally forced herself to call David's office on Wednesday to give him some price estimates and ask when he could squeeze in a meeting at the hotel hosting the banquet and auction, she was almost childishly relieved to learn from his new receptionist that he was unavailable and would be for the rest of the day.

"You could try catching him on his cell phone between his visits to prospective clients," Jasmine suggested, "but the best you'll probably do is voice mail."

"Thanks," Serena said as she hung up. Voice mail worked for her. Much as she had once enjoyed talking to David, she wasn't entirely sure what to say to him yet. Price estimates, she reminded herself. *Keep it professional.*

She took a deep breath and dialed, prepared to sound proficient and detached when she left her message.

"David Grant speaking."

Ack! Was it too late to hang up, or did his cell phone have caller identification?

"Hello?" he prompted.

"H-hi. It's Serena, I wasn't expecting to talk to you."

"Ah, you meant to call another man?"

She leaned back in her desk chair. "Jasmine said I would have a tough time getting through to you."

He muttered something that sounded like "Ironic," but added in a clearer voice, "Well, whether you intended to or not, you got me."

Refusing to read anything into his words, she said crisply, "Great. Then we can discuss meeting times. Although I can easily messenger over the program samples and—"

"That's a pointless business expense when we'll need to get together to discuss other issues anyway."

Scowling into the phone, she thought that one little across-town mailing wouldn't break the bank. She hoped. "All right. I gather today's out of the question. What about to—"

"I have a conference call with our contracts department in the morning, and those boys who only speak legalese can be long-winded. Then I have lunch with Nate Filcher, the CEO of Digi-Dial, a company we're trying to partner with. I have a callback interview in the afternoon for some-one to help our HR department. And Friday's even worse. It'll be tough to fit you in."

Well, don't do me any favors, she thought, grinding her teeth. This was *his* project, after all, the event he'd hired her for at the last minute, insisting he be part of the planning.

"Look, David, if it's too much trouble for you—"

"Any chance we could have dinner?" he asked. "I could pick you up—"

"That won't be necessary," she interjected quickly, hav-ing learned her lesson yesterday. "As it happens, I have an appointment downtown late tomorrow afternoon." He wasn't the only one with a schedule. "Why don't I just meet you somewhere?"

"Great." The background noise suddenly dulled some, and his tone became brisker. "I'm here, so I have to run. I'll have Jasmine call you to finalize the details."

He hung up before she had a chance to respond, and she blinked at the dismissal. And the irrational hurt over feeling insignificant, bumped down from David's busy and important priority list to something his receptionist could follow up on. What was wrong with her? She was accustomed to working around a client's schedule. To some extent, they paid her to be available at their convenience. It wasn't something she took personally.

Of course, she'd never slept with a client before. Good thing she wouldn't be doing it again.

No more confusing business and pleasure, she told herself as she slid into a restaurant booth the following the evening to wait for David. Mixing the two was as volatile as crossing friendship with sex. They didn't necessarily blend, and as great as the sex was, the possibility of losing one of the few people she'd been able to depend on for years was too great a price to pay.

She watched the entrance, not really sure what to expect from today's meeting. They'd both been highly annoyed when they'd parted ways two days ago…but the annoyance had come after both being highly aroused. Had he meant what he said about not even *mentioning* sex? That should make him easier to resist then, right?

Wrong. The second she spotted David enter the restaurant and start threading his way toward where she sat, her heartbeat started to race and her insides quivered. Every single cell in her body was attuned to his presence and clamoring for his attention.

Nothing's changed. He wasn't the man for her, she wasn't the woman for him. But her warning went unheeded. Stupid cells.

"Hey," David said as he dropped onto his side of the booth. "Been waiting long?"

She shook her head, unable to find her voice. Surprisingly, even more than she wanted to kiss him hello, she wanted to apologize—tell him she didn't mean to keep leading him on and pushing him away. But they'd laid the sexual issue to rest, and digging it back up seemed like the textbook explanation of dumb.

A waiter bustled by, taking their drink orders and asking if they wanted an appetizer.

"Artichoke dip okay with you?" David asked.

The cheesy dip, actually baked inside a loaf of bread, was one of her favorites. Hardly low cal, but why not take this opportunity to add on a few pounds? No one was going to be seeing her naked anytime soon.

"Bring it on," she told the waiter, who raised his eyebrows at her glum tone.

"Rough day?" David asked once they were alone.

His blue eyes held genuine concern, and she knew that he was ready and willing to listen to any problems she had. He'd be so much easier to resist if he was grouchy with her, or smug in the you-don't-know-what-you're-missing-baby kind of way. The trouble of course was that she knew *exactly* what she was missing.

"No, it's just been a long week." That was a nice, nonspecific way to encapsulate the turmoil of the last few days.

He nodded, his expression sympathetic. "You know what's great for tension? A massage. I know some people are shy about it, but the reward for letting go of your hangups is definitely worth it. Nothing melts your problems away like the right person's hands on your body."

The right person's hands on her body was what had

caused her problems in the first place. "I don't think so," she said, reminding herself that this was business. Picturing her customer naked was inappropriate.

"What about just indulging in a weekend spent in bed, then?"

She bit back a groan. "I, um, have plans this weekend. In fact..." She hoped Alyson had been right about inviting David. Serena had to do something to get them back on track as friends. "Are you busy Saturday?"

His eyes got so wide she was glad no food had arrived yet. Judging by the apparent shock her question had caused, he undoubtedly would have choked, and performing the Heimlich would have necessitated her touching him. Which couldn't possibly be a good idea.

"Why do you ask?" he wanted to know. "Business or pl—"

"Neither. I mean, pleasure, I guess. There's a birthday party for my friend Alyson. I've told you about her."

"The yoga instructor, sure. And you want me to come along?"

"Not as my date!" That really couldn't be stressed enough. "But you're new to Atlanta, and we're friends, so I thought... But I completely understand if you're too busy." After all, the man's belongings were still locked in storage while he worked too hard to find a place to live, and he'd just barely been able to make time for Serena this evening.

His jaw had tightened somewhere between "not as my date" and "we're friends," but he managed to smile anyway. The result was grim. "I wouldn't miss it."

Figured.

"Oh." She forced a smile of her own. "Well, great. I know Aly really wants to meet you."

The waiter returned with their appetizer and David's frosty lager. Serena barely waited until the bread bowl was on the table before ripping off a piece and plunking it in the hot dip. Bread and cheese were comfort food, right?

David watched her silently, gallant enough not to comment on her uncharacteristic feeding frenzy. A moment later, she acknowledged that appetizers weren't what she was hungry for and pushed the plate closer to him. She lifted a navy-blue folder from her seat. This was a business meeting, after all, and discussing the fund-raiser was the safest thing for her to do. Both in terms of her emotional state *and* staving off possible future cellulite.

"I got your e-mail with the final list of bachelors," she told him, flipping over the printout where she'd jotted down the combined number of men available in all the participating companies and her suggestions for time periods. "I'll give you my ideas and let the guys decide amongst themselves which they want. They can choose from my selections or brainstorm their own, but I need an answer fast if they need me to track down costumes. Here are three sample programs for the event."

He lifted the one in the center, with fiery orange text on slate-blue paper. The words *Time to Find A Cure* were centered, encircled by *from the dawn of time to a limitless tomorrow* in a smaller font.

"I like where you're going with this one," he told her. "I'll take a quick majority vote tomorrow morning, get you the specific information for the inside, and hopefully you can send the order to the printers before the weekend."

With so many tiny details that had to be ironed out, Serena had plenty to distract her from the simmering attraction she was trying to ignore—even if, while they discussed the number of seats, she was more interested in the man seated across from her. His eyes crinkled at the corners every time he smiled at her, in a sexy, mischievous expression that made her want to lean across the booth and kiss him. The faint scent of an expensive, masculine cologne washed over her like a warm, seductive breeze, and it was difficult to imagine ever returning to a platonic friendship.

Could they do it?

Something sharp and panicky jabbed her in the heart. Surely it wouldn't always be this way, with her so aware of him she was ready to come out of her skin. It was good that she'd invited him to the party on Saturday. Maybe being around other people would take some of this intimate pressure off and help them relax with one another again. Maybe being around some of her more off-beat friends would open David's eyes to the fact that Serena was comfortable in a much different world than his.

With any luck—she'd be sure to wear her earrings—by the time the party was over, they'd be back on the right track. As opposed to the how-soon-can-I-get-you-naked? track where she was currently circling in fruitless laps.

UNDER different circumstances, Serena grabbing his hand and tugging him behind an oversized easel in a dark corner might have given David hope. Somehow, that wasn't the case Saturday night in the dimly lit art gallery. For one thing, there were about three dozen other people in the spacious front room, and not even his free-spirited Serena was quite that exhibitionist. Also, since she'd given him a list of reasons why he should just meet her here rather than their driving together, he was pretty sure she wasn't angling to get him alone. No, her actions probably stemmed from the fact that he'd gone in today for "a few hours" and had unintentionally worked until almost dinner time, only arriving moments before the expected birthday girl.

"You're late," Serena chided, her soft, husky voice a caress all its own even though she'd let go of his hand and was carefully not touching him.

"I got caught at work," he whispered back.

"On a *Saturday?*"

"In my defense, I would've been here sooner, but I didn't realize 285 would be backed up."

"Oh, come on—285 is always backed up! But I'm glad you made it." She sounded almost surprised about being happy he was here.

So why had she invited him? He thought he knew the answer to that question. Serena wanted to prove they were friends—safe, platonic friends who could go thirty seconds without wanting to tear each other's clothes off. Delusional. He'd be surprised if she could make it twenty, and his personal best was eight-and-a-half.

A rustle of murmurs went through the crouching crowd in the gallery's main room, a passing on of "I think she's here" interspersed with "shh"s.

The front door opened. Illuminated by the outside lights, a woman and her taller companion stood on the steps. On cue, everyone yelled, "Surprise!" and appeared from behind urns and a reception desk and the sign stating exhibition dates.

An inside light flipped on, and David got his first look at Alyson Kane, a petite woman with almost waist-length dark-red hair and a beatific smile. She pressed a hand to her heart and laughed in delight, but as she scanned the room thanking everyone for coming and exclaiming over how shocked she was, he caught her send a sly wink in Serena's direction. Then the woman's gaze slid from Serena to David himself, and she advanced in his direction. Her date followed, but stopped to say hi to some acquaintances.

"Happy birthday, Aly!" Serena sidestepped David to hug her friend.

"Thanks. So, am I finally getting to meet David?" The woman's expression was friendly, but judicious.

He realized he was being assessed, and it suddenly occurred to him how important it was that Serena's friends not find him lacking. "David Grant. It's a pleasure to meet you. Serena's told me a lot about you."

"Same here." Alyson said, her eyes twinkling with mischief.

He slanted a look in Serena's direction, and discovered she was blushing, from her cheeks all the way down to the neckline of her asymmetrical top. Her shirt, the color of lime sherbet, was held together at one shoulder by a beaded multicolored butterfly, then the material draped at an angle over her breasts, toga-style, leaving her other shoulder completely bare. As if that tantalizing glimpse of skin wasn't enough to raise his rocketing temperature, the material stopped at her midriff, exposing her smooth, flat abdomen. The tiny blue crystal shimmering at her navel coordinated with the butterfly.

His gaze fell to her black jeans as he gauged how difficult they'd be to remove.

"David!"

Serena's sharp tone caused him to glance up guiltily. Perhaps her definition of platonic friends didn't include undressing each other with their eyes? Pity.

"There's someone else I wanted to introduce you to," she told him, waving her fingers at Aly as the birthday girl dutifully went to mingle with her guests.

Right, he was very interested in meeting people...as opposed to tossing Serena over his shoulder and finding someplace where they could be alone.

Afraid he was eyeing her like the big bad wolf with Red Riding Hood, he tried to focus on something neutral. "So, how surprised do you think she was?"

Serena laughed. "On a scale of one to ten? Not very. Come on, you have to meet Craig."

Another male artist type. David ground his teeth together, hoping Serena didn't decide to try dating this guy now that Happy was out of the picture.

A lanky man with dark hair and an eyebrow ring appeared in their path, shaking hands with David and engulfing Serena in an enthusiastic hug. The chances of David ever becoming friends with the guy increased drastically when Craig pulled back and grinned at a nearby pretty woman with a shy smile.

"Serena, this is my incredible girlfriend, Emma Baldwin. Em was a little nervous about meeting you, so no third degree."

Serena sniffed. "I wouldn't dream of putting her on the spot. Besides, I thought it would be more fun just to tell her lots of embarrassing stories about you."

Emma laughed, but Craig narrowed his eyes in mocking retribution. "Oh, really? And does David here know all—"

"It's lovely to finally meet you, Emma," Serena interrupted.

"Same here," the other woman said. "But I almost feel like I know you already. Craig speaks so highly of you, and of course I've seen his work, so—"

A strange croaking emitted from Serena's throat, making her sound a lot like the little frogs outside in the velvety spring night. She coughed. "Sorry. Throat's scratchy. Who wants a drink?" she asked brightly. Or manically, one might say.

"We're good," Craig said, nodding toward the glasses of wine they both held. "But the bar's set up over in the corner. I should go wish Aly a happy birthday."

David followed Serena, wondering where conversation would have headed if she hadn't discovered a sudden thirst. Someone had turned on a sound system along with the overhead lights, and a strange ethereal music reverberated through the open space, accompanied by a much earthier electric guitar and occasional drum.

"That's interesting," David commented, tilting his head to listen.

Serena pursed her lips. "It's a demo tape from someone Aly knows. You don't like it?"

"No, it's good. Different. Has an otherworldly grace, a sort of untouchable quality." He ran his gaze over her. "But there's just enough lusty, good old-fashioned rock and roll there, too."

"It's surbahar," she told him as they stood in the short line at the bar.

"Su-ba-who?"

"A bass sitar."

"That would mean more to me if I knew what a sitar was."

"You know sitar. Remember that Indian restaurant with live music I took you to the last time you were up for Christmas?"

He'd always arrived for his visits with her in a state of amused anticipation, never knowing for sure where she'd drag him next but confident they'd have a great time. "Actually, Serena, I was here for Christmas a few months ago. But you were avoiding me then, remember?"

She bristled. "I was not. I told you, I was busy with work."

"Yes. That is what you told me."

"I can't believe you of all people would give me grief about this. *You* were working today, on a Saturday!"

"This relocation is important." In fact, if he hadn't been seeing her tonight, he very well could have worked another few hours. He fully intended to be AGI's youngest vice president ever and make his family proud, not that they weren't already, but still… And Lou Innes himself had a trip to Atlanta scheduled soon to check on David's progress.

"Having a place to live is important, too," she argued. "You didn't think today might be a good time to continue apartment hunting? Then again, if you're going to live at the office, anyway, I guess an apartment is irrelevant."

"That's ridiculous."

"No, it's not. Do you realize every time I called you in Boston, I reached you at the office? No matter what day or time it was, I knew odds were best I'd find you there."

He wasn't sure what to say to that. Yeah, he worked long hours. But she made it sound as if he didn't have a life, which was nuts. He'd gone to his share of sporting events and even the theatre…of course, he often went with business connections. He dated often, too, although more than one woman had complained about his demanding schedule.

"What can I get you, buddy?" A dark-skinned man with a lilting foreign accent waited expectantly for their drink orders.

David requested a beer, and Serena took a bottle of water. She scanned the crowd, and he suspected she'd find more people for him to meet. And he wanted to, really, but not as much as he wanted to savor a few moments with her alone.

"So, can I get the tour, or is the rest of the gallery off-limits?" he asked.

She lifted an eyebrow. "Didn't think you were much of an art enthusiast."

"Just because I'm not one of those people likely to plunk down thousands of dollars for a blue triangle on a black background doesn't mean I have no sense of culture. Besides, since when do you pass up a chance to broaden my horizons?"

"Fair enough. Come on, then." Winding her way among the other party-goers, she led David out of the high-ceiling room and into a side corridor lined with stands displaying gleaming pieces of three-dimensional art, some depicting images of the jungle or the ocean, others far more abstract.

"Blown glass," she told him. "These are all part of a traveling exhibit, done by a man in Oregon. Gorgeous, aren't they?"

They truly were. He tended to associate glass with being clear and colorless, but the artist had trapped a rainbow of color in the smooth pieces. The corridor circled around to a staircase, leading to a second and third floor that looked down on the expansive lobby area. She pointed upward to a suspended sculpture that was clearly the artist's rendition of the sun, even though it was made up of violets and blues instead of yellow or orange. David hated to imagine the destruction if the spiky spherical piece ever fell.

On the second floor, Serena led him through a room of canvases painted with acrylics, growing animated enough in her admiration for the artwork that she forgot to be tense because they were alone together. Unfortunately, he was so captivated by the sparkle in her eyes and flush of pleasure that he was uncomfortably aware of their intimate isolation. The buzz of conversation below seemed to be part of a different world.

"You ever think about it?" He nodded toward a picture that was somewhat harsh in its use of bright colors, but arresting nonetheless. "Pursuing art of some type?" Instead of pursuing the artists she so often dated. David knew her mom had "dabbled" in several mediums, and that Serena herself had worked nights at a community arts center when she was first trying to get her company off the ground.

She smiled ruefully. "My father would just love that. I spend all that money on a business education and then 'blow it' chasing a dream. Trying to make a living as a creative artist would actually make what I'm doing now look lucrative."

Her father? It was so jarring when she made comments like that, because she didn't seem at first glance to be the type who'd care too much about what others thought. But Serena was more vulnerable than people who didn't know her might guess.

"You deserve to be happy. And you're an adult. Who

cares what your dad thinks?" The subject of James Donavan often set David's teeth on edge, because he'd been on the consoling end of more than one conversation about her father, who might want what was best for his daughter, but who often approached it in a brusque, uncompromising manner.

Her laugh held an edge to it. "*You're* going to tell *me* to disregard family opinion? Then I suppose you're not at all concerned with living up to older brother Ben's distinguished career in politics. Or proving anything to the older generations of Grants?"

He stiffened. Sometimes he forgot that knowing her so well was a mutual thing. "All right, I admit there's a lot of pressure growing up a Savannah Grant. We succeed, period. And I want not only to succeed, but to show I can do it well on my own merits. But I'm not letting that run my life. I enjoy my job."

"Sorry, I got defensive." She ran her hand over his arm in a conciliatory, innocent gesture that still made his pulse quicken. "As it happens, I enjoy my job, too. I party for a living, don't I? I get to be my own boss instead of answering to a committee of suits or dealing twenty-four seven with corporate politics…. Besides, all my attempts at artwork turned out looking like something I would proudly display on my refrigerator if I had a two-year-old."

David blinked. Serena with kids? Shockingly domestic, but she was so loving and nurturing that any child would be lucky to have her as a mother.

"What?" she asked. "You're looking at me weird."

"I had a weird thought," he confessed. "You ever think about having a family?"

Her eyes grew wide, almost panicky. "Not really. Maybe

sometimes I—no. None of my relationships ever got serious enough to start discussing that kind of future, and even though some women might make it work, after growing up with Tricia, I'm not eager to do the single-mom thing."

He tilted his head to the side, considering. "Now that you mention it, none of your relationships ever did get all that serious, did they?"

That had certainly never bothered him, since he hadn't liked half of her boyfriends anyway. But it was interesting to think about now, especially since he'd only just started noticing her antsy reaction to things like family and home and long-term commitment.

"I imagine your parents' divorce turning ugly left its share of emotional scars," he added, wishing he could erase any past pain she'd suffered.

"Please." She snorted. "*Yours* are happily married, and I didn't see you popping the question to any of your past lovers."

"None of them were the right girl. Guess I was waiting for someone else."

She swallowed. "Well…good luck finding her. You know what? Your party conversation sucks. Let's get you downstairs where you can get more practice. If you're going to move to my town and start hanging out on Saturday nights, you'll have to stop being so serious."

Patience. Finesse. "You're the events expert. Lead the way." He wanted to get past whatever fears she had about giving them a chance, but he didn't want to push her into the arms of the closest waiting poet, painter or Greenpeace volunteer. Not that David had anything against those men…so long as they stayed the hell away from Serena.

He followed her down the curved staircase, trying to rein in the sudden feeling of possessiveness and struggling not to be too obvious about the fact he was ogling her ass in those jeans.

When they reached the main room again, David saw that the party had mostly split into two factions. The larger group had taken over the lobby as a makeshift dance floor. A smaller cluster of people, including Alyson and her date, as well as Craig and Emma, sat to the side in some padded folding chairs and were passing around an oversized book.

Serena headed in the direction of her friends, and David was perfectly happy not to have to dance.

Alyson glanced up with a sly grin. "Hey, wondered where we'd lost the two of you."

"Not lost, appreciating the artwork upstairs," Serena said.

"Well, now you're just in time to appreciate the artwork down here," said a man David hadn't been introduced to. "We've been looking at Craig's portfolio. We're trying to get Zach to book a showing."

"Zach manages this gallery," Serena explained, even though David had sort of put that much together on his own. "He's the one in the red silk shirt, dancing."

David had to admit he didn't usually feel so stodgy in his wardrobe, but his chambray button-down rolled up at the sleeves and his khaki slacks made him the odd man out at this shindig. He nodded around the circle as Serena introduced the remaining strangers—Wes, the man who'd spoken, Summer and an attractive young woman named Billie.

"I'll go grab a couple of chairs," Serena said.

"I can do that," David protested.

"And I can't?" She laughed. "Don't worry about it. Stay, get to know everyone."

Someone handed him the oversized binder of Craig's sample work, and David took it almost absently, watching Serena and still trying to perfect that not-ogling expression. He glanced down politely, thumbing through some sketches and realizing they were good. Really good. How did Craig create such a sense of motion in a drawing of a window, a clear sense of golden sunlight in a black-and-white medium? David flipped a page, recalling Serena's comments in passing about her "starving artist" friend and trying to think if there were any commercial opportunities he could offer someone of Craig's talent. Suddenly one image leapt off the page at him and David couldn't breathe. Serena, naked.

Now there was something he hadn't expected to see tonight.

9

WELL, IT WAS official. She was going to have to take Aly and Craig out back and shoot them.

Serena had walked back to the circle, lugging a couple of chairs, in time to see David's eyes go the size of potters' wheels. And she'd realized very quickly why. *Damn.* In the sketches Craig had done of her, she'd had her head turned and almost none of her face was visible. Lots of people could stand next to her and look at one of the finished paintings, never realizing it was Serena in them. But to say David knew her body intimately verged on understatement.

Why did they have to show him that?

She should probably wait until it wasn't Alyson's birthday to throttle her for not interceding on Serena's behalf. Not that Serena was embarrassed about posing, just that she'd been making a concerted effort to keep the "David" and "nudity" areas of her life separated. She tried to recall if Billie, Wes or Summer knew she'd been Craig's model for the Contemplation series. She hoped that Alyson and Craig would be tactful enough not to remark; Emma obviously knew it was Serena, but she was the least likely to speak up in group conversation.

Serena set down one of the chairs with a thunk.

"Good timing." David's eyes met hers. "I need to sit."

A brief electric moment passed between them, but then he flipped to another drawing. "Craig, you've got some amazing talent. Don't get me wrong, I draw a mean stick figure myself, but these are incredible."

"Thanks." Craig beamed in Serena's direction. "Feel free to bring him along whenever we get together."

More time with David? Just what her sanity needed.

The techno-blues song that had been playing wound down on one last soulful note, and Zach gave up dancing in favor of sauntering toward them. "Alyson, love, I have to leave for South Carolina distressingly early tomorrow morning for the art festival, so how about we move on to cake and gifts now? I don't want to miss your oohing and aahing over what I got you."

Oohing and aahing was probably an accurate prediction. Zach was known for selecting fabulously extravagant presents.

"You don't have to twist my arm." Alyson laughed, waving her arm toward the gyrating party-goers. "Let them eat cake!"

"I've got candle detail," Serena said, scooping up Craig's portfolio and carrying it far, far away from David's curious eyes.

The Red Velvet cake Serena had picked up this afternoon was back in a small concessions room where gallery guests could buy coffee and pastries. Alyson joined her only moments after Serena had flipped up the light switch.

"Hey, shouldn't you be out there, guest of honor?" Serena asked.

"I wanted to count the candles, put to rest the ugly rumor floating around that I'm twenty-eight. Let's not age me a year before my time."

"You're lucky I don't tell everyone you're twenty-nine."

"Thought you looked perturbed." Aly grimaced. "Sorry. So many people here are familiar with Craig's work, it didn't even occur to me beforehand that you might not want David to see the pictures. After all, it's not as if he's a stranger to you without clothes."

True. Serena didn't know why she was feeling so sensitive. Was it because of the heat that had flooded his gaze, encouraging a rebellious answering heat inside her? Or just because she was waiting for him to be judgmental about her stripping in the name of art? David could be more conservative about some things than she was, and she didn't want an argument on the subject to strain their friendship. As if repeatedly making out with him then pushing him away hadn't done that already.

She stabbed a candle into the cream cheese frosting with enough force that the only thing left showing was the wick. Oops. She managed a smile for Alyson. "You should go open your presents."

"You're sure?"

"Absolutely. I'll be out in a sec, just as soon as I get all the candles on. It was thirty-two, right?"

"Funny. I can't imagine why you don't have your own stand-up act at the Punchline."

Alyson vacated the doorway, but the sudden solitude gave Serena time to ponder the conversation she'd had with David upstairs. What had *that* been about? She didn't know all that many hot guys her age who cornered women alone at parties to ask them about motherhood, of all things.

It was just one more illustration of how she and David were different. Her "plans for the future" included keeping her business alive and kicking through the next financial quarter, and David was thinking about things like the next generation of Grants. Of course he was. With the possibility of being made a vice president and now only being a few hours away from his family, he'd start to consider finding the right woman. Someone who would make a good executive's wife, someone he could take home to Mom and Dad.

The thought gave her a pang, and she shook herself mentally as she carried the cake into the other room. Everyone sang and clapped for Alyson, then Serena stood at the lobby desk, cutting pieces of cake for other guests. Most wandered off with their paper plates, but David made himself comfy in the sleek black chair behind the desk.

"Thanks for inviting me tonight," he told her.

"Glad you could make it." Sort of. She finished dishing up her own slice of cake, then leaned against the desk, facing him. "I hope you're having a good time."

Having just stuck a forkful of the rich dessert in his mouth, he didn't answer, simply looked up and locked gazes with her. Her heart beat a little faster at the unreadable expression in his eyes. Was he sorry he'd come? Did he like her friends? Did he wish something had happened when he and Serena had been alone upstairs?

Did *she*?

He swallowed. "Craig's very talented."

Since he kept his tone neutral, so did she. "I couldn't agree more. His work's been reviewed in several magazines and newspapers, he's just waiting for his big break."

"In the meantime, I'd love to help him out any way I can. Think he'd sell me 'Nude with a Navel Ring'?"

Her tummy clenched, in a combination of nerves and

something far more tingly and pleasant. "I believe the piece you're referring to is called 'Repose.' And I, ah, don't know that it's for sale. Some things were just meant to be appreciated, not owned."

"That's a shame." His eyes swept over her, from her face down her sensitive breasts and abdomen to her legs and sandaled feet. "I really don't think I can put into words how much I want her."

She set her plate on the desk. "All right. Say you bought the finished painting or the original sketch, where would you put it? At the office? In an apartment you haven't even found yet? I'm having trouble picturing just where she'd fit."

He clucked his tongue. "I always pegged you as having more imagination than that, Serena. Isn't that what makes you good at your job?"

"Yes, but...not everything should be work."

Strangely enough, she thought of her father, and the last time she'd seen him and Meredith. Whatever personal differences Serena had with her future stepmother, the woman made James Donavan happy. Serena couldn't remember her parents ever being happy. She'd heard tales that made her think they'd been drawn together with an immediate, fiery passion that was a sight to behold, but that spark must have burned out when she was still very young. What she remembered was how hard they'd worked to change each other.

And how bitterly it had all ended. Too bad James had married Tricia first and spent all those years being miserable, instead of waiting for someone like Meredith. Too bad Tricia, as was her way, had thrown herself into their relationship headfirst without stopping to think maybe they just weren't right for each other. That's what they'd both needed, for someone to say, "You know what, this is a mistake."

"Now *you're* the one who seems too serious for a party," David said. "Want to dance?"

"With you?" Maybe she should have worked harder not to sound horrified. But she and David, close physical proximity, the pulsing beat…? Nothing about that spelled wise decision. "You don't even like dancing."

"True. But I would do it for you." His expression made it clear that dancing would be almost as painful a sacrifice as taking a bullet for her. But she had no doubt he'd do it.

Her body moved without mental permission, and she leaned forward to reach down and squeeze his hand. "That's sweet. But unnecessary."

The contact was just enough for him to brush his fingers over hers, and warm chills quivered through her body. She tried to pull back, but for a second he refused to let go.

"David…" *You promised.*

"All right." He released her and stood. "Let me know when you change your mind, Serena."

She supposed there was no chance he was referring to the dancing.

"Hey." Natalie looked up from her desk as Serena walked into the office, the second to arrive for a change. "How was your weekend?"

Tortured probably wasn't the adjective Natalie was expecting. "Fine. Had that birthday party for Alyson."

Natalie nodded. "Sorry I couldn't make it. Previous plans and all."

"She understands, but she says you still owe her a gift," Serena kidded.

"So." Swiveling back and forth in her chair, Natalie inspected her French manicure. "Did you take a date?"

"Nope." Now would be a good time to quit chitchatting in the outer office and get to her own desk. She had plenty to do.

"Really? Because when I met Alyson for lunch yesterday to present her the certificate to Spa Sydell, she said David was there Saturday."

Ambushed! "I invited David to go because he's my friend and I thought he might like to meet more people in Atlanta." Not that Serena could quite picture David on his days off hanging out with Craig or Zach. For one thing, it would require David taking days off. "He wasn't a date."

"Oh." Natalie looked disappointed. "So he didn't seem interested in you at all?"

"Hey! Who said *I* was interested in *him*?"

Natalie rolled her eyes. "Please."

"For your information, I'm not. Do you know what he brought up when we were talking Saturday? *Kids*. Families, marriage, suburbs. He actually thinks about stuff like that."

"No! The horror. Nothing worse than a hot guy capable of acting like a mature adult. Give me a smarmy commitmentphobe any day."

So much for the who-needs-men? solidarity. "I think you're forgetting who signs your paycheck."

"Fine, fine." Natalie raised her hands in front of her. "No need to threaten the poor assistant's livelihood. Just forget I said anything, and I'll get back to work."

"Good. I'm going to do the same." Or make an attempt, anyway.

The errands that demanded Serena's attention would probably go more smoothly if she could get her mind off

David, but, short of exorcism, she wasn't sure what more she could do in that regard. Hadn't she spent all yesterday trying not to think about him?

Resisting thoughts of him—resisting the man himself—had been a lot easier when he'd lived in Boston. Then again, not thinking about David would also be simpler if half the tasks she had to do this morning weren't for the auction. Maybe she shouldn't have taken on the fundraiser, but there had been too many reasons to say yes and no real logical one for refusing.

Luckily, despite her preoccupation, plans were coming along smoothly. The programs were being printed, most of the bachelors being auctioned had costume fittings scheduled, arrangements for the actual banquet would be finished this week and publicity was coming along nicely. In fact, if it weren't for the fact that she and David were supposed to pay a visit to the hotel tomorrow afternoon, she might even be able to relax a little and concentrate on her other clients.

When her personal extension buzzed shortly before eleven, she had the brief hope that it would be David telling her he couldn't make it the next day and that she should go on to talk to the hotel management without him.

"Serena Donavan speaking," she answered.

"Oh good, Serena, I reached you." Meredith's anxious voice came over the phone line. "I needed to talk to you about the wedding."

It was bizarre how often her future stepmother needed to talk about the wedding, considering Serena had absolutely no formal role beyond daughter of the groom, yet these calls increased in frequency the closer they got to the June first ceremony. A few weeks ago, Serena had fielded a hysterical call about napkin rings. Maybe the antsy bride had already alienated those closer to her, and Serena was the last resort as crisis hotline.

"What can I do for you, Meredith?"

"Tell me whether or not you have an escort. You RSVPed for two," she explained. "So we used that for the head count and seating charts and all the other plans, but as your father was just pointing out last night, you're between men again."

Interesting coincidence that every time Meredith called, Serena got a migraine. Honestly, her father had never really liked anyone Serena had dated, yet after a breakup, he managed to make it sound as if the split was due to a defect on her part.

"So I worried that you were attending solo." Meredith babbled on, oblivious to the fact that Serena was enjoying this conversation almost as much as that time she'd accidentally slammed her finger in the file cabinet. "Which would be okay, I suppose, but it'll throw off the reception arrangements. And of course *my* children will be with their respective spouses…"

Meredith's daughter, Eliza, was a doctor, and her son, Martin, had a PhD in economics. Naturally, both of the overachieving freaks were married. Oops. What Serena had meant was, in addition to succeeding in their chosen fields, her soon-to-be step-siblings had also found time for meaningful relationships.

"I'll have someone with me," Serena assured the nervous bride. "Hey, who understands better than me the nightmares of unbalanced seating at a big event, right?"

Meredith sighed in relief. "I told your father you'd take care of it. But you won't bring that man with all the body piercings, will you?"

All the piercings?

"Craig? He only has one." Fewer than Serena herself, though presumably Meredith didn't object to pierced ears. "I'm not sure who I'll bring, actually."

"Oh." Meredith's breathing took a turn toward hyperventilation, as though it were napkin-ring trauma all over again.

Good grief. *Do they really not trust me to pick a suitable escort?* Serena was a little surprised they hadn't given her tips on what she should wear to the nuptial gala. Perhaps that was next week's call. *Stay tuned for Serena's Inappropriate Wardrobe.*

"It'll be okay, Meredith. I'll find someone you'll love." Unbidden, the image of David flashed behind her eyes.

"Actually, dear, what your father and I want is for you to find someone *you'll* love."

"Th-thanks." Serena blinked. Even though she knew James and Meredith did try, in their own way, to express affection for her, these unexpected moments of caring were difficult to process. She really shouldn't be so cynical about their attempts to reach out to her. "That means a lot to me."

"I'm glad. Neither one of us wants to see you end up like Tricia, in her fifties and gallivanting aimlessly around the world with men half her age."

Considerably less choked up with emotion, Serena slapped a hand over her eyes. "I promise not to bring anyone half my age." For one thing, she had no interest in teenagers.

Come to think of it, she hadn't had much interest lately in grown men, either. At least, not in any man who wasn't David Grant. And if she didn't find a way to exorcise him from her system, she didn't know what she was going to do—besides go quietly mad from distraction and perpetual lust.

SERENA THOUGHT maybe it was a good thing she was with David this afternoon and not some other client who might have given up on her and fired her half an hour ago because of her inability to focus. Then again, if she'd been with anyone other than David, she wouldn't be suffering from this inability.

He sat in the armless Italian-style chair close to hers, his arm casually draped over the back of her seat. Her body buzzed with his nearness and the familiarity of his cologne. The smell brought back memories of David holding her close and moving inside her, taking her to new heights. Gee, and she wondered why she was having trouble concentrating?

Luckily, the hotel manager they'd been talking to had had to interrupt their conversation to deal with a guest crisis, giving her a moment to regroup. Except that the man's absence left her alone with David.

"What are you doing after this?" David asked, leaning in her direction.

Taking a cold shower. "Just heading back to the office to tie up some loose ends on other projects."

Since the hotel was located more or less between their two offices, they'd agreed it made the most sense to meet here.

"Can you spare a few minutes? I just realized you've never seen where I work," he pointed out. "I'd love to show it to you. The view's incredible."

"I don't know…"

"I have the finalized printout of silent auction items for

you. I forgot to bring it with me." He gave her a boyishly apologetic smile.

Convenient. The man was so...well, *manipulative* seemed harsh. He was just determined. And resourceful. Traits she admired, unfortunately.

"David, if you want me to go to your office, all you have to do is ask. You don't have to resort to 'forgetting' documents."

"I *did* ask. So you accept? If you want, we can even order sandwiches from the deli in the building's lobby. It'll be almost six by the time we get out of here, so you might as well stay with me until after-work traffic dies down."

She blinked, trying to replay the situation in her head and figure out how they'd gone from immediately parting ways to her sparing a few moments to see his office to now having dinner together. "I probably won't be all that hungry. As soon as you sign off on those papers, we get to do the fun part."

"Really?" The word sizzled out of him like a stray bolt of lightning.

She hastened to add, "We have to finalize dessert selection for the banquet menu. It's pretty much the last thing on our to-do list." At least, the last part he'd be directly involved in, thank the good Lord.

"Dessert-tasting, huh? Well, it's tough being the chairperson for the event, but someone had to do it."

Did he know what a sucker she was for that grin? Even when they'd been in school, dating other people, she'd looked forward to making him smile, seeing the way his mouth quirked up and his eyes sparked with mischief, watching his lips—

"Serena."

She jerked her gaze up to meet his. "Sorry. Did I space out?"

"You were staring."

Staring. Right. Considered in most civil circles to be rude. "My mind just wandered. I hope I didn't make you uncomfortable."

"You have no idea how uncomfortable." *But I wouldn't mind showing you,* his heated expression said.

She shifted in her chair, nervously tucking a strand of hair behind her ear.

"Hey. Your lucky earrings."

Despite her inner tension, Serena smiled that he remembered. She'd bought the turquoise earrings in college at a spring Renaissance Festival some friends had dragged her to when she should have been studying. She'd invited David to go along, but he had insisted his chances of taking the business world by storm would be better if he didn't bomb his finals. A woman in gypsy garb had given Serena a spiel about the inexpensive stones bringing good fortune to the wearer, and it hadn't taken much more than a B+ on an econ exam to convince Serena.

She'd worn the earrings today because, knowing she'd be spending hours with David, she figured she'd need all the luck she could get. The slight click of the doorknob made her turn around, and she beamed at the returning hotel manager.

After blinking at what was probably the most blatant expression of relief he'd ever seen, the man returned her smile. They finished negotiating costs for such ballroom extras as a microphone and use of a stereo, with Serena frequently pointing out that this was for a charitable cause, then the hotel manager stood. "If you'll follow me to the dining room, we have an excellent dessert sampling set up for you."

As they walked down a carpeted corridor, David nudged Serena. "Good work back there."

The pride in his voice sent a flush of pleasure through her. "Just doing my job."

"You do it well. I knew I was right to put myself in your hands."

"I aim to please my clients. But you should probably withhold opinion until the night of the auction, when you see how it all turns out."

"Yeah. I'm pretty curious about that."

She glanced in his direction, and their gazes locked. The night of the auction. His imposed deadline. Would he really give up on her if she managed to keep her hands to herself for the next couple of weeks, find someone else to lavish with his sensual attention?

It was what she wanted, after all. For both of them. Still, the image of another woman in David's arms caused Serena's steps to falter.

He reached out to take her elbow in his hand. "All right, there?"

"I'm great." Aching at the thought of him making love to someone else, she snapped, "Absolutely *great*."

He cocked his head, wisely letting go of her. "Hey, you don't have to convince me. I always thought you were."

Terrific. He was going to be nice even when she was practically snarling at him? No wonder she was crazy about the guy.

Don't think like that.

The manager pointed them down the steps into the sunken, candlelit dining room, which wasn't yet crowded with dinner guests, and excused himself. A waiter stood next to a table covered in crisp white linen. He pulled out a seat for Serena, and she started in surprise when David sat next to her. There were four chairs, and she'd been expecting him to sit across from her.

The farther away he was, the easier she breathed. When he was this close, her body felt softer, fuller somehow, more responsive to trivial stimulations she wouldn't normally notice. Her thighs seemed hypersensitive to the brush of her broomstick skirt against her skin. She hadn't bothered with the confinement of a bra under the thick weave of her short-sleeved sweater, but now she regretted the oversight. Each slide of the fabric over her bare breasts was like a caress from David himself.

"I figured it would be easier to reach everything if I sat here," David said.

Blinking away the image of his reaching for her breasts, she conceded he probably had a point. The miniature dessert servings were arranged on rectangular pieces of crystal, each in a dish on its own lace-edged doily. It was a scale-model feast for the senses—tiny but scrumptious rations of fruit-garnished crème brûlée, dark chocolate mousse cake, raspberry sorbet, tiramisu, carrot cake and key lime soufflé.

Serena's mouth watered at the tantalizing variety. "Wow."

"Enjoy." The waiter handed them each a set of silverware wrapped in cloth napkins and left them to their gourmet orgy.

"If anyone ever asks me my favorite part of the job, this is definitely it," Serena added.

"So, what do we attack first?"

He had to ask?

"Chocolate. Definitely the chocolate." She'd barely

placed her individual portion on her plate before raising a big forkful. Moist, spongy layers of sweet and semi-sweet cake surrounded rich mousse so dark it verged on bitter. The contrasting flavors exploded in her mouth in a decadent taste that made her moan.

David watched her, looking hungry but not touching any of the food. "That good, huh?"

"You hafta try this," she muttered, running her index finger over her bottom lip to catch any of the filling she might have missed, and wolfing down the rest of her piece.

It was gone too fast, and she shot a covetous glance at the remaining sample.

David clucked his tongue. "You didn't savor yours and now you want mine?"

"Just one more bite," she lied.

"That's really going to be enough to satisfy you?" he asked.

No. Not even close. "You know what, you take it. There's plenty more here."

He lifted his serving of the soufflé from a plate drizzled with kiwi syrup and powdered sugar.

She couldn't believe he'd passed over the cake. "Aren't you going to try the chocolate?"

He laughed. "Some of us enjoy saving the best for last and taking our time."

"I like instant gratification," she muttered.

His clear eyes turned smoky with intensity. "There are times when that's pretty good, too."

She swallowed. "Speaking of good…how's the soufflé?"

"Not bad." He finished it, but he didn't seem rapturous about the dessert.

"I assume it didn't make the cut for our guests?"

"Definitely not. I mean, it was okay. Just not that special something, you know?"

She knew. What happened when you knew exactly what special something you were yearning for, but couldn't have it? At least, not beyond the short term.

Move on. She took a bite of the raspberry sorbet, mostly to cleanse her palate before she inhaled one of the other desserts. But it was surprisingly delicious. Sharp, tart, addictive. As each spoonful liquefied on her tongue, she found herself immediately craving more.

"We should make this one of the two choices," she advised David. "A good light dessert women especially can enjoy without guilt. But more than that, it's fantastic. Here."

She lifted her spoon, and he cupped his hand under hers, guiding her to his lips instead of simply taking the piece of silverware. His fingers slid softly against hers, and a small spasm of desire pulsed in her stomach. His warm breath against her skin had her melting faster than the sorbet.

"Incredible," he pronounced.

With a soft breathy sigh, she pulled her hand away, as disappointed not to be touching him anymore as she was relieved.

"You know what I just realized was missing?" David asked, surveying the desserts with a critical eye.

"Missing?" Was he kidding? She glanced at the table. Throw in a harp and some halos, this was her idea of heaven.

"Come on, you grew up in Georgia!" He grinned at her. "Pecan pie. We had a housekeeper who used to make the most amazing recipe. You would've loved it. It had a touch of chocolate in it."

"I can't believe with all this in front of you, you're thinking about pie."

He met her eyes. "Tough to settle for substitutes when you know what you really want."

"I…" *Pretend he's any other client, and not someone who causes you to wake up sweaty and aroused in the middle of the night, twisted in your own sheets.*

"Never mind. I'm not trying to be one of those difficult customers demanding more. Guess I just had a moment of nostalgia for pie. The simple things in life, right?"

Sure. Except that his "simple" life had included servants, a guest house and stables.

He tried the carrot cake, declared it marred by the unfortunate presence of raisins, and shared her admiration for the crème brûlée. She tried to follow his suggestion of savoring the delicate crunch of caramelized sugar, but it dissolved away into nothingness too quickly. After he'd taken a cursory bite of the chocolate cake, he gallantly pushed the plate toward her, giving up the rest of his piece. *Savoring, shmavoring,* she told herself as she greedily consumed it. Why deny herself what she wanted?

She glanced over to where David had closed his eyes as he enjoyed the tiramisu. Why, indeed?

"We have a winner," he murmured huskily, sounding like a man overcome with ecstasy. He gestured to the other serving with his fork. "Try yours."

"I don't know." She'd been a little nervous about spending the afternoon with David and hadn't eaten much for lunch. Mini-portions or not, this was a hell of a lot of sweets on an empty stomach. Turns out you *could* have too much of a good thing.

"You don't have to finish it. But, as my official consultant on the dessert matter, would you just taste a little bit?"

"All right, but only because you're paying me."

As she'd done earlier, he lifted a fork to her mouth, and she dutifully tasted the sweet delicacy. *Mmm.* Wow. The full-bodied creamy dessert with just the right bite of espresso was indescribable. She ran her tongue over the metal tines, making sure she got every last bit.

When she finally managed to speak again, she raved, "I've found my bliss."

David chuckled. "So, this and the sorbet are our final choices, right?"

"Absolutely," she said. "This is…this is beyond words. I can't believe it's better than the chocolate cake. I didn't expect to like *anything* better than the cake."

It surprised her that even as well as she knew herself, without David's prompting, she would have made the wrong choice. Even though she'd acknowledged moments ago that she'd probably had enough dessert to last a lifetime, she couldn't resist finishing the last morsel of tiramisu. But then she really did groan. Good thing she hadn't worn slacks—the zipper would have self-destructed two bites ago.

"No more," she declared.

"Don't worry, there isn't any." He indicated the empty plates, bare except for the decorative drizzles that served as memorials.

"I meant no more *ever*. I may have cured my sweet tooth once and for all."

"I know what you mean. I think I did the same thing with root beer when I was younger."

"Think you could ever have too much pie?"

He brought his finger to his chin, considering. "Hard to imagine ever having too much, but yeah, I guess maybe I could if I gorged myself."

Perhaps that was the secret. Instead of denying yourself, indulge in what you wanted until you no longer wanted it. Could it really be that simple?

Why not? She clung to the idea with the frantic optimism of a desperate woman. Nothing else had worked.

10

"WANNA TAKE the stairs?" David asked, his body feeling restless and on edge.

"To the *eighteenth floor?*" Serena slanted him a look as the elevator doors opened onto his building's lobby. Though she didn't actually call him a raving lunatic, she might as well have.

"Right." He followed her inside. "Just a thought. You know, to help burn off the desserts."

The desserts—twenty minutes of the most excruciating torment of his life. Did she know what the tasting had been like for him? Listening to her little murmurs of delight, watching her eyelids flutter closed as she all but purred in satisfaction? The image of her running her tongue over her lips in greedy enjoyment was vivid in his mind.

The doors parted again in the AGI suites, and David and Serena almost ran smack into Larry Bell, a fellow Boston transplant who worked in finance and was walking with his head down as he read a report in a green folder.

"Oh, sorry," Larry muttered as he glanced up and stepped to the side. "I wasn't expecting anyone to be getting off on this floor. Most everyone else is headed home. But I guess if anyone was going to come back after hours, it would be you, boss."

David stiffened, aware that Serena already thought he was a good candidate for workaholics anonymous. "I'm just ducking in for a few minutes, to show Serena the new offices. Larry Bell, Serena Donavan. She owns Inventive Events."

"The company arranging the benefit? A pleasure to meet you." The tall blond accountant closed his folder and beamed at her, his smile revealing a bit too much appreciative interest. "I can certainly see why David volunteered to put in so much extra time on this."

David's jaw clenched at the man's flirting. Didn't Larry know bean-counters were supposed to be reserved, quiet and—when at all possible—*geeky* introverts?

"Thanks," Serena said. "But I think David's just dedicated to making this auction the best it can be, as am I."

"Well, I'll do my part. I'm one of the bachelors," Larry clarified for her. "Representing ancient Greece, so next time you see me, I'll probably be in a toga and wreath, carrying an abacus."

"A number cruncher no matter the time period, eh?" David gave his colleague a tight smile. "We should stop holding you up before the elevator goes back down without you."

Larry nodded, a dawning understanding in his green eyes. "Sure thing. I look forward to seeing you at the auction, Ms. Donavan," he added from behind the closing doors.

"He seemed nice," Serena said.

"Oh, yeah. Larry's a gem." David took a deep breath, but it did nothing to ease the knot of possessive tension in his stomach. Maybe he should get Serena to his office before she ran into any other bachelors who made David want to gnash his teeth. "This way."

Larry was right—most employees of the not-fully-staffed future headquarters had gone for the day. Cubicles were deserted, and lights were off in all but one or two offices. The floor was quiet, except for the murmur of a few behind-closed-doors conversations and someone running copies on the machine.

He stopped at the corner office and pulled the keys out of his jacket pocket. "This one's mine."

"Wow." Serena passed him as he flipped the lights on and shut his door.

He grinned, knowing that the view from the floor-to-ceiling window was impressive and glad he'd been able to talk her into coming up to see it. "Nice, isn't it? I'm getting so spoiled that I've started looking at penthouse apartments."

She turned away from the skyline just enough to smirk at him over her shoulder. "Oh, so you aren't planning to live in a corporate efficiency suite indefinitely?"

Her wide-eyed sarcasm made David feel a little defensive. His mother had given him a similar minilecture about his "homeless" situation when he'd called his parents last week. *And Serena didn't think she'd have anything in common with my family.*

"Hey, getting this office up and running smoothly was a big task. Until Richard moves down next month, everyone comes to me with their questions, and preparing for the transfers from other offices was like a full-time job itself, on top of the new client solicitation they actually pay me for and the necessary extra schmoozing like the benefit. But you'll be happy to know I've got appointments this week at a couple of buildings with new vacancies."

"Good." She gave a quick nod of satisfaction. "I hope you find a home soon."

So did he. What he was paying in storage was ridiculous.

The thought gave him pause, as convenience was generally a higher priority for him than cost. Serena must be rubbing off on him. He hung his jacket on the coat tree and crossed the room, the largest office he'd ever had. Mahogany bookshelves matching his desk lined the far-side wall, and slate-blue carpet covered the floor. He just hoped that when Lou Innes arrived next week to look things over on the partners' behalf, he'd think David was doing a good enough job to warrant the great office and increased responsibilities.

Stopping next to Serena, he glanced out at the buildings that reflected the golden glow of a gradually descending sun that wouldn't truly set for another couple of hours. "You should see it at night," he told her. "The view's more amazing then."

Almost immediately, he wished he hadn't pointed out that he was here after dark, which didn't come until eight or nine around this time of year.

"Really?" She pressed her hand lightly to the glass. "Hard to imagine it being any more spectacular."

He glanced at her profile—her warm brown eyes, stubborn chin, lips that haunted his dreams. "It's just buildings. There are all kinds of things I'd rather be looking at."

Inhaling sharply, she angled her face up toward his. He leaned forward reflexively, wanting so badly to kiss her. *You gave her your word.* That's right—he wasn't going to make a move in her direction for two more weeks. And if she didn't make one in his… Maybe he'd been an idiot to spout that ultimatum, but he was geared for problem-solving strategies that got results and that had been what he'd come up with in his frustrated-as-hell state.

Needing space between them, even if it was only a

few feet, he walked toward his desk and dropped into the expensive swivel wing chair, then spun around to face her.

Lifting her arms in a quick stretch, she moved away from the glass and followed after him, apparently not understanding that he'd walked away for her own good. He was attempting to respect her "professional boundaries," instead of making love to her in a way that proved she was off-limits to moon-eyed accountants and any other men drawn to her. Her standing in front of his chair wasn't helping.

"Like what?" she asked with a sassy smile.

"Excuse me?" he asked, too busy with his struggle to keep his hands off her to process her out-of-the-blue question.

"You said there were other things you'd rather look at," she prompted. "So I was asking for an example."

He blinked. Serena might have been blissfully unaware that the entire time they'd savored dessert samples, he'd been thinking about the way *she* tasted or that he'd had an irrationally possessive moment when he could have smacked affable Larry Bell upside the head with this year's tax code, but Serena wasn't an idiot. *Is she flirting with me?*

The woman who'd repeatedly told him to keep his distance? Probably not. But it was worth exploring.

"Artwork's always good," he said slowly. "There's a specific piece I wouldn't mind looking at every day while I was in my office…but I doubt I'd get much work done."

Her breathing quickened. "Did it bother you? My sitting for those pictures?"

"*Those?* You mean there was more than one! Hell yes, it bothered me." Concrete evidence of her sitting naked in a room with another man was a particularly sore spot at the moment, since she was so adamantly opposed to getting naked with *him*.

"Forget I asked," she said, a brief cloud of sadness passing over her face before she grinned. She sauntered toward him, adding a little extra swivel to her hips. "Why worry about a picture when you could have the real thing?"

Okay, this went way beyond flirting.

The woman was seducing him! Hot damn. He couldn't have felt luckier—or more shocked—if he'd won the lottery.

As soon as she was close enough, he reached forward to encircle her wrist in his hand. "You've changed your mind?" What had finally won her over?

The playful light in her eyes flickered. "Not my mind, David, just the rules."

Something sharp grated against his insides—dread and a rusty, unfamiliar sense of defeat replacing the bright burst of optimism. "What do you mean?"

"You gave me until the night of the auction, and that's what I'm willing to give you. A hot, short-lived fling that ends after we're not working side by side anymore and you won't be driving me so crazy I can't sleep at night."

"Serena." He had no idea what to say. The part of him that realized he'd just been given the green light to have sex with her wasn't all that interested in the part of him that was surprisingly irritated. And hurt. He'd had meaningless affairs before. That wasn't what he wanted from her.

"It wouldn't work between us," she said. "Not for long. But you want me and despite everything I've tried or told myself, I want you. Badly. This was the only way I could think of to have my cake and…well, you know. Let's just say I'm hoping that indulging myself helps me kick the craving."

Did she honestly believe that two and a half weeks would be enough to slake the passion between them?

She ran a palm along his cheek, her smile rueful. "You're not used to having to compromise on your goals, I know. But this is all I can offer you and still protect myself."

Protect herself from what—*him?* "I wouldn't hurt you."

"That's not a guarantee anyone can make. Two people can start out with the most sincere, passionate intentions, and still…" She started to draw back. "Take it or leave it." His hold tightened involuntarily. He wasn't about to give her up, even if the only way he could have her right now was to agree to this ludicrous proposal. He'd negotiate the fine print later.

He pulled her down toward him, meshing his fingers in her hair as he ground his lips against hers. His hungry kisses held a slight edge of anger. He thrust his tongue into her mouth, wanting to make her desperate for him, telegraphing his own arousal and willing her to share its intensity. She moaned, and he tried to drag her into his lap. The confined shape of the wing chair made it difficult for her to straddle him the way they both would have liked.

She turned her head, her breath coming in shallow pants as he traced his teeth along the curve of her neck. "The…chair won't work."

It could, actually, if she were to sit in his lap facing the other way, which brought to mind intriguing possibilities. But for another time.

With one arm around her, he pushed his weight up with the other so that they were both standing. As soon as he had his balance, he reached for the elastic waistband of her skirt and tugged, drawing a shaky laugh from Serena.

"What happened to savoring?" she asked as the material pooled around her high-heeled sandals.

"If I only get two and a half weeks," he said as she slipped the buttons of his shirt free of their holes, "I'm not wasting time."

He reached between them, sliding his hand under her sweater. The discovery of her bare breasts and their taut nipples caused his erection to flex against his fly. He yanked the top up over her arms. Serena standing in front of the skyline in a pair of heels, aqua-blue underwear and a gold belly ring—now *there* was a sight that rivaled anything in the Louvre.

"And you didn't think the view could get any better," he murmured as he lowered his head to her chest.

He drew on one peak, curling his tongue around her. Suckling, nibbling, alternating sides. Serena writhed, her hands tangled in his hair, shifting her weight from foot to foot. As much as he loved her breasts, the urge to touch her elsewhere was too great to be ignored. He went down on his knees, tracing a path with his mouth down her abdomen to her belly button, flicking his tongue over the ring there.

Clasping her hips, he sank lower in front of her, level with the smooth V of her panties, inhaling the perfume of her desire. He hooked his fingers in the string sides and peeled the underwear down, stopping midthigh, just enough to reveal her to his sight. And touch. And definitely taste.

He scraped his fingers lightly over her and parted the plump outer folds of her damp skin, so dark it was almost purple. Beneath, she was even slicker—hot and wet to his touch as he teased her inner lips with the pad of his thumb, leaning forward to run his tongue over her. Her erotic, musky flavor was far more tantalizing than anything they'd tasted earlier. Serena was shifting more restlessly now and instinctively trying to spread her legs farther apart, incapable of doing so because of the panties.

"Patience," David teased, moving his mouth against her as he uttered the word. He found the swollen bud jutting out between the intimate creases of flesh and sucked on her. Hard. She gasped his name. Drawing back, he ran his tongue over her again, lightly, soothingly.

"Screw patience," she said raggedly. "I want you inside me. *Now*."

He half obliged her with two of his fingers, moving in and out of her as he continued to make love to her with his mouth. Her legs sagged into his chest for support, and moments later, she tightened around his hand and began quaking in a rhythm that seemed to match his pounding pulse. Her body went as limp as a rag doll's, but he knew he could give her even more. She just had to let him.

Cupping her bottom, running his thumbs along the round, smooth underside, he bent forward again, laving her with his tongue, capturing her still-pulsing clit. She squirmed, not quite voicing her half murmur of protest. He knew all her nerves were extrasensitive right now, but that was precisely why, if she just gave him a minute...

Fighting his own body's demands for release, he sucked on her, barely scraping his teeth against her as he slid his finger inside her, bending it so that his knuckle pressed right against that sweet spot that caused her to explode. His name erupted from her in a near-hysterical shriek as her body convulsed. She practically toppled against him. The sheer force of her orgasm almost sent him to his own climax.

Supporting her, he lurched to his feet, unzipping his pants with one hand, and spun her trembling body toward the edge of the desk. She turned her perfect round white butt up toward him as she braced herself with both hands, and he yanked the panties down the rest of the way, not caring if he ripped them in the process. It took agonizing, interminable seconds to find the square packet and roll the condom over his straining erection.

Serena was dizzy with sheer need. She'd never felt so on fire before, and though she should be beyond sated, she felt empty. She was dying for David to be inside her, to be part of her and give her the very specific satisfaction only he could. After already coming so hard, it wasn't an orgasm her body demanded, it was *him*.

Pressing her palms to his desktop, she imagined him here behind the desk tomorrow, thinking of her, of this. He gripped her hips, and she gyrated, thrusting up toward him, trying to hurry his entry. She felt him brush against her, taking his time. She whimpered and rocked back.

With a muttered oath, he surged forward in one fierce stroke that filled her completely and stole her breath. She almost collapsed under the weight of sensation, her arms bowing slightly and her chest pressing forward enough that her nipples rasped along the sharp edge of the desk. The friction only added to the sensual desperation she felt. Struggling to regain just enough coordination to meet his pace, she pushed up on the balls of her feet.

Sweat beaded on her forehead, and she bit down on her lip to keep from shouting out encouragement that would carry through the building—in case there was anyone left who hadn't heard her the last time. Keeping one hand anchored on her hip, he reached around in front of her with the other. Starting where their bodies were joined, he moved up to her clitoris, circling it with his fingers until her womb clenched and her back arched.

Her body moved with a will of its own, bucking frantically as her world fragmented and her orgasm pulsed through her all the way to her pointed toes. A moment later, he grasped her with both hands, hauling her up against him as he shuddered in release.

It was like an astral experience. Feeling as if she'd actually floated above herself, Serena rested her head on the desk, wondering if she'd ever regain feeling in her legs but not really giving a damn. A dazed moment later, she realized David was pulling her into his arms. They sank to the floor together, her cradled against his chest, and she drifted off, cocooned in a blissful stupor. Eventually, he kissed her.

She tasted the salt of perspiration on his lips, and smiled, her body still wobbly with the aftershocks of their lovemaking. "That had to have burned off at least a few calories."

He chuckled tiredly, leaning back with his head against the side of the desk and closing his eyes. "It's settled. I'm signing a lease on a place this week."

Bold, yet random. "Oh-kay."

He opened one eye. "I want your help breaking in all those rooms."

Limp as she was, she already looked forward to it. "I see. So you've just been missing the proper motivation."

"Right." He squeezed her butt. "Think you can provide it?"

"My pleasure." The understatement of the year.

"*Admit it.*" David glanced up from the box he was taping with a smirk.

How was it that even the man's smirks were sexy?

"You didn't think I could find a place this fast," he said. Serena had stopped underestimating him—and his ability to pay extra for a speedy move-in—ages ago. "Well, I didn't realize you *Fortune* 500 types were so impulsive." He'd told her the building he was visiting had immediate vacancies, she just hadn't known *immediate* meant two days after first seeing the place. When he'd come to her loft for a few hours Wednesday evening, it had been to tell her all about the apartment he'd just seen and to have dinner.

They hadn't covered many of the apartment specifics, and the pasta had been ice-cold by the time they'd remembered to eat.

"We *Fortune* 500 types prefer *decisive.*" He leveled a pointed look at her. "I know what I want when I see it. And I go after it."

She shivered, but definitely not because she was chilly. They'd spent most of last night "going after it," yet she was still ravenous for him. Too bad she had to leave in the next few minutes. David had taken off the whole day to meet the movers over at his new place, but she had client errands that had to be completed later today. And she still had to run by her apartment. Sleeping over at his efficiency-apartment hotel—not that much sleeping had occurred—had been unplanned, and no way was she going to work in the slacks and peasant blouse she'd worn yesterday.

Serena applauded spontaneity, she just wished she'd been better prepared for how right it would feel to wake up in David's arms this morning. And how alarming that sense of cherished belonging would be. Right now, however, with his eyes on hers as he walked toward where she sat on the bed, the last lingering traces of alarm melted into a swirl of longing.

At the sound of a muffled ringing, he sighed, his expression one of regret, and turned away. He glanced around the efficiency apartment, basically just a room with a shoe-box-sized kitchen in the corner and an even smaller bathroom. "Any chance you've seen my cell phone?"

She looked around from her vantage point. Since she'd finished helping him pack up the clothes in his closet, she really should have left, but she'd been sitting on the mattress admiring the biceps revealed by his T-shirt as he worked.

"Uh, we used it to order Thai food pretty late," she recalled. "Check around the kitchen."

That proved good advice, and a moment later he was frowning into the receiver. "That's ridiculous. We had a verbal agreement with them. Okay, I'll come in. Just give me…" He glanced at his watch and swore, then cupped the receiver with his hand. "Serena, you know I'm supposed to meet these movers. Is there any—"

"No." She might not wear a suit or have stockholders, but she did run a company and had real commitments.

"Right, sorry." He flashed her such a charmingly repentant grin that her annoyance was short-lived. Back into the phone, he said, "Just give me time to unlock my place for them and give some general directions on where to drop the furniture. I'll get to the office as soon as they've cleared out. In the meantime, see if Jasmine can set me up a lunch with Digi-Dial's CEO."

He looked so vexed when he hung up the phone that sympathy tugged at Serena. "I'm gonna go out on a limb and guess that wasn't good news?"

"We've been hammering out the so-called final details of a deal with Digi-Dial, a cell phone company. A *big* deal. We were going to sign a contract for their using our technology in all their products, and it's something I personally put in a lot of hours to secure for AGI. But the rumor is they signed with a competitor of ours this morning." He ran a hand through his already tousled dark hair. "Damn, this is bad timing. Lou's coming down next week to monitor my progress. I want this fixed by then. Or to have something even bigger and better in the works."

She slid off the mattress and crossed the room to give him a quick hug. It was probably the first touch they'd shared in three days that didn't pulse with a sexual undercurrent. "Hey, piece of cake for a *Fortune*-five guy like yourself."

"Thanks." He flashed her a quick grin, then paced away. "Change of plans, though. I don't think your coming by the new place this evening makes much sense. I'll be working late."

Disappointment seared her, along with the panicky thought that they were losing precious time. "But…there's not much you'll really be able to do in the middle of the night, is there?"

"There are all kinds of things I should be doing," he corrected her. "Researching prospective partner companies to replace Digi-Dial, putting together a report for Lou on the progress we're making in our new sales areas, and making a few phone calls to other time zones. But don't worry, tomorrow, I'm all yours."

"Tomorrow, I have that parachute wedding, remember? Here comes the bride…from four thousand feet."

"I can't believe that's how you're spending your day." He scowled. "What a ridiculous way to get married."

"I'll have you know, I busted my butt to make this ceremony and reception fabulous." If you could call something that took place on the tarmac a reception. "I even arranged for binoculars for each of the guests waiting below."

"I'm sure you did a great job. But come on, is that really what you picture when you think of your own wedding?"

She blinked. Her wedding? Ha, that was a good one! "Who said I want to get married? And frankly, I think it's commendable that they thought outside the box and did something a little different than the white veil and rice on the church steps. But obviously *you*—"

"Whoa." He held up his hands. "We took a wrong turn somewhere. Just because AGI is having a crap day is no reason we should. I wasn't trying to be critical, I'm just upset about blowing this deal."

"I know. And I didn't mean to get snippy." She sighed. "Guess that makes me a bad...friend."

"Let's make it up to each other." He pulled her against him and pressed his lips to hers in a kiss so brief it was no more than a tantalizing tease. "Will you have time tomorrow night, after the sky-diving service?"

"I'll make time," she promised. They kissed again, with considerably more thoroughness, but Serena decided if she didn't pull away now, neither of them was going to get done the things that required their attention. "Tomorrow. Your place. Call me with directions?" She recognized the upscale area of town from the address he'd mentioned, but she needed a specific route.

"Definitely. I don't want to lose my one and only volunteer for naked unpacking."

She laughed. "I didn't realize the two were concurrent when I made my offer."

"We'll negotiate tomorrow." He winked at her as he walked her to the door. "You won't be able to miss the place. Shiny new building, big fountain outside."

Naturally. Because David would never move into a funky renovated complex with faulty air-conditioning located in a loud neighborhood. Making her way across the parking lot, she told herself that it was a good thing he would be living on the other side of town. This way, she ran little risk of running into him after they said goodbye.

We'll still be friends, though, she reminded herself. Just from a safe distance.

Lots of people maintained relationships from a distance. How often did she see her own mother? For that matter, how often had she seen Patrick when they'd been dating? And it wasn't as if she'd had a particularly serious or successful romance even before Patrick. *I'm not good at relationships.* Which was why David would thank her in the long run for not having one with him.

11

When his cell phone rang Saturday evening, David actually jumped in his seat, and not just because it was clipped to his waist and set on vibrate—he'd turned off the volume during his earlier meeting with Filcher's right-hand man. The good news was that Nate Filcher, Digi-Dial's CEO, had not officially signed with AGI's competitor...but they were discussing contract options. David needed to meet with the man again, but Nate himself was out of town for the weekend.

Now, David was racing back to his apartment, which he'd planned on unpacking today, at least enough that he and Serena could have a nice, relaxing evening. And sheets. But Nate's second-in-command was long-winded, and David hadn't realized how late it was. So it was with extreme guilt and trepidation that he answered his phone.

Please don't let her have beat me to the apartment. "Hello?"

"David! It's your father." If Blake Grant's physical appearance had become slightly less powerful in his sixties, his voice certainly hadn't. It radiated the same immediate authority as always.

"Dad, this is a surprise." When David had called home with his new address and pending phone number, the housekeeper had informed him that his mother had decided last minute to join David's father on a business trip abroad. "Tara said you were in Paris."

"They have phones in Paris," his father said matter-of-factly.

In the not-too-distant background, a female voice urged, "Find out if Tara was right. Does he have a roof over his head now?"

"I don't think he was living on a street corner in the meantime, Lily," Blake muttered to his wife.

"Still, I did not raise my boys to be transients."

"We raised them to work hard, and David does that. It comes with some sacrifices."

"Benjamin's going to be in *Congress*," Lily pointed out, "and he makes it over for an occasional Sunday dinner."

That was because David's older brother lived right there in Savannah. He'd never particularly struck out on his own. And why, David wondered, had his parents placed an international call if the bulk of their conversation was going to be with each other?

"Dad, I appreciate your checking in, but—"

"Wait. Your mother wants a word."

Of course. "Hi, Mom."

"I'm so excited you finally took the time to find a place! Can't wait to see it. We purchased our tickets for the banquet, and Tara says they arrived in the mail. I was really hoping that you'd have time to come down to Savannah some time before the charity event, but—"

"It's been crazy, Mom."

"I know." Her voice softened with maternal affection. "Just don't work yourself too hard. Benjamin wants us all to do some family pictures for the media before his campaign gets into full swing, and he'll be crushed if you look skeletal with dark circles under your eyes."

He laughed, knowing she was needling him. "I'll keep that in mind."

"Good. Then we'll see you later this month. And for pity's sake, try to unpack before then. I'd rather not discover you're still living out of boxes."

A frisson of anticipation went through him. "Actually, Serena's coming over to help with that."

"Ah. The mysterious Serena. We'll finally get to meet her, won't we?"

"Definitely. The auction is really her baby as much as mine." But a cold shadow passed over his heart as he answered. He'd like to introduce Serena as the woman in his life, but if she was to be believed, their affair would be over by the night of the auction. There'd been moments during the last few days when she'd looked at him with so much emotion in her eyes that he'd held his breath, certain she'd finally realized that what they shared was stronger than her fears, only to have her dance away, out of reach—emotionally, anyway.

Her deadline loomed nearer. If Serena was worried about their differences, intimidated by his upbringing or position, he would just try harder to show her that she could fit into his world.

SERENA RESISTED saying anything to the doorman about the suspicious glances he kept sending toward her and her red canvas tote bag, but really, what did he think she was going to do? Steal the ugly and uncomfortable mauve-and-gold-striped chair she'd been waiting in?

But she'd made good use of the last fifteen minutes,

coming up with a few choice words for one David Grant. After the sky-diving ceremony she'd spent most of the day orchestrating, she'd headed as quickly as possible for her apartment to change into something casual enough for unpacking and old enough that she wouldn't care if it was ripped off her and pack a few things in case she stayed the night again. She'd missed David last night with such fervor that she'd been in a lust-motivated rush to be with him.

She wouldn't have hurried if she had known he wouldn't even be here.

The security in his building was such that she could come inside, but to use the elevator, guests either had to have a key pass or be buzzed up by the resident. When there had been no response from David's apartment, she had explained to the doorman that David was expecting her.

The man's already skeptical expression had turned positively disdainful. "Mr. Grant," he'd informed her, "has been out since noon."

He had invited her to wait in the lobby, then proceeded to glance her way every few minutes as if she was a psychotic ex-girlfriend he should perhaps protect Mr. Grant from. If David ever bothered to show up, she could show them psychotic. Where *was* he? The man had promised to get a head start on his apartment today, so that they could spend time together this evening, not that she minded helping with the unpacking. She had fun with him no matter what they were doing...as long as she didn't get preoccupied with wondering what would happen when their affair was over. It would hurt, she knew that, but she didn't regret the decision she had made in his office. Sexually speaking, they had already opened Pandora's box; Serena was just giving them some time to enjoy it, to satisfy their craving and move on.

Unfortunately, being with him had been more like feeding an addiction. But right at the moment, she was annoyed enough to think that maybe she *would* be able to move on with her life and find another man. One who didn't stand up his dates. Sure, it was only fifteen minutes—going on twenty, now—but what really angered her was that she had no way to gauge how much later he would be. He couldn't have called to let her know? She had a cell phone, for God's sake! When she'd tried his, she had only received his voice mail, so his phone was either busy because he was talking to a client, or it was turned off because he was with an important client. Either way, it wasn't hard to see where Serena fell on his priority list. Knowing the hours he kept, she wondered if this was standard modus operandi for how he treated his girlfriends.

But you're not his girlfriend.

Just as she was reminding herself of this, David strode into the building, nodding and already waving off the doorman who approached to tell him he had a visitor. Her tardy date was wearing Saturday business attire, khaki slacks and a dark golf shirt, but his face was slightly flushed and his hair fairly disheveled, considering its length. Man, she was a sucker for him when he looked tousled. *Cut it out*, she told her hormones, *we're annoyed, remember?*

"Serena, I am so, so sorry. I lost track of time, but then I was hauling ass back here, trying to decide if I should call you or not and my phone rang."

She pressed her lips together. "An important business call, right?"

"No, actually." He held out his hand to help her up, and she thought about not touching him, since he was sure to win her over faster that way, but there was no reason to be petty. "My parents. From Paris. I couldn't just hang up on them."

If either of her parents thought to call her from abroad, she wouldn't just brush them off, either. Of course, she probably wouldn't be able to carry on a conversation because she'd be so shocked to hear from them, but that was another story. To be fair though, her mom had sent her a hastily scrawled postcard a couple of weeks ago to inform her that Bolivia was wonderful, as was Antonio (who'd apparently replaced Miguel).

David took her tote, shrugging it over his shoulder. "Mom was going on about me finally finding a place to hang my hat, it's a miracle, hallelujah, and then talking about family portraits for Ben to use in his campaign press kits. You understand, right?"

Only in the abstract, she thought as they walked to the elevator. She suspected if Meredith's son, for instance, were to run for office, no one would phone the stepsister in the art district to request her presence in family photos.

Suddenly David glanced from the bag he carried to Serena, and a broad grin lit his face. "Does this mean you're staying over?"

The pull of attraction was far stronger than the grudge she'd been trying to work up. "I was thinking about it."

"You mean before I kept you waiting?" He pulled her into his arms as the elevator moved up. "Stay with me. Then I'll have all night to make it up to you."

What woman in her right mind could resist an offer like that?

SERENA never would have guessed that her "perfect place" could be an overpriced apartment suite that was home to a talking coffeemaker (a gift, he'd sheepishly explained) and enough business suits to open a men's clothing department. But, lying on her side Sunday evening across David's king-size bed with him snuggled against her back, one strong arm locked around her bare midsection, she was feeling dangerously content. Happy, sexually sated— for the moment—and perhaps more at peace than she'd felt since she'd learned David was moving to Atlanta.

David nuzzled her shoulder, his weekend version of a five-o'clock shadow brushing her skin. "You asleep?"

"Uh-uh. You promised there'd be food later." She turned to grin at him. "I don't want to waste away to nothing, you know."

His blue gaze ran over her body. "Nope, can't have that happening."

He seemed so relaxed that her smile widened. Even though he'd been happy to see her last night and had lived up to his promise to make her waiting worthwhile, for the first hour or so she'd been here, he had obviously still been tense about his work dilemma. It had been gratifying to see his preoccupation replaced by desire.

"You look good like this," Serena observed. Nicely rumpled, grinning, with a manly hint of stubble along his hard jaw. "You're one of those guys who somehow makes scruffy very sexy."

Although *one of* was a ridiculous way to put it, because David was in a class by himself.

He kissed her knuckles, then dropped another kiss at her collarbone, slowly turning his head so that his cheek scraped over her skin. "It doesn't bother you? Not too scratchy, or anything?"

"I like it rough," she teased.

His eyes glinted with wicked mischief. "Definitely filing that away for later. The way you're looking at me now, it'll almost be a damn shame to shave again. But somehow I doubt AGI would share your appreciation for the scruffy image."

She snorted. "Like facial hair really impacts a person's job performance."

Sitting up, she glanced around for her shirt, or one of his. Anything she could wear while rummaging his badly stocked kitchen for food. "Did *any* of our clothes actually make it back to the bedroom?"

They'd made love in several other places first, before showering together and falling into his bed.

He waggled his eyebrows at her. "You don't have to get dressed on my account."

"One appetite at a time, slugger." She glanced at the floor again. They'd unpacked a fitted sheet and slept under his comforter, but the matching ivory bedsheet was still lying at the top of a nearby open box. She reached for that and wrapped it around her. "I have this fantasy that I'll get to the kitchen and little elves will have left groceries."

"Hmm." He knelt by his side of the bed and retrieved a pair of shorts from somewhere. "*I* was sort of hoping for a starring role in your fantasies. I'm disappointed to hear it's elves instead. Don't worry. Assuming they didn't stock the pantry, we'll order out."

"Again?" She recalled his apartment in college—a considerably cushier place to study than the library or her dorm, but he'd never had anything edible on hand. He'd generously sprung for countless pizzas, though, pretty much the staple of David's university diet. "You know it would be cheaper if you ever just bought groceries."

"Cut me a break. I may not have the assortment of fresh produce you're always replenishing, but I'm in the middle of a move here."

"And you do more cooking when you're *not* midmove?"

"Well." He glanced down sheepishly. "They say time is money, and I work a lot of hours, so when you look at… What?"

"Nothing." She tried forcibly to smooth away the scowl she could feel on her face. Why was she feeling cranky all of a sudden? The reminder of his scheduling priorities, the reminder that they had a different perspective on money? Or just low blood sugar? "Let's go see what we can get delivered in this neighborhood of yours. Unless you want to pick something up."

"I hadn't planned to leave the apartment. That requires your really getting dressed." His gaze trailed over the bedlinen spooled around her body. "I'd be perfectly happy for you to wear even less than that for the next two weeks."

Her laugh was strained. "That might make Dad's wedding awkward." Correction, more awkward.

The wedding! As David padded out of the room, she realized she'd never followed up on her rash promise to Meredith to find a suitable escort. *Invite David.* He more than qualified.

Not a chance.

But why not? In times past, she would easily have asked him for the favor, assuming he didn't already have social plans with some coiffed heiress sorority chick. She tried to picture him among Meredith and James's guests—her dad's workaholic younger brother, Meredith's supersuccessful kids, tons of country-club members Serena wouldn't know. David would fit in effortlessly.

What a depressing thought.

Heaving a sigh, she joined him in the kitchen, where he'd pulled an assortment of brochures, menus and other literature out of a black folder. She raised her eyebrows. "One day in the apartment and you've already amassed all that information? I mean, I knew you were organized, but..."

"It was in my welcome packet."

Ah. Of course. When she'd first moved into her loft, she'd been given two keys and a warning that the tattoo place on the corner overcharged.

"What are we in the mood for?" he asked. "Seafood? Barbecue?"

She wrinkled her nose. "Barbecue tends not to be vegetarian-friendly."

After they finally decided on pizza, she laughed, thinking that some things never changed. *And some do.*

While physically, this newfound freedom to explore her attraction to David was the ultimate in sensual enjoyment, emotionally it made her feel helplessly vulnerable. Growing up, she'd often felt distanced from others. Unlike most of her classmates, she'd had no siblings, her grandparents had all lived out of state, her mother was caught up in starring in her own life movie, and James fretted whenever his daughter laughed too loudly in an inappropriate situation or wanted to run barefoot.

Serena had had friends, sure, but she'd gotten used to a certain distance in her relationships. As close as she and David had become, they'd kept things platonic until now and had dated other people, which provided a feeling of safety. Was that why she'd never consciously acknowledged how drawn to him she was in college?

She stared out the glass sliding doors on the other side

of his sunken living room. The skyline twinkled in the growing darkness, making her somehow feel small and overwhelmed. While David placed their order, she wandered onto the balcony. The air was so soft against her skin that she didn't even mind the warm humidity. Being outdoors had always made her feel more balanced. She had a little patio at her place, too, but it was a concrete slab that looked out onto the parking lot. Certainly not a generous deck with enough space to house a state-of-the-art gas grill and a padded rattan chaise longue.

A few seconds later, she heard David's footsteps behind her as he disconnected the call. "Isn't it great out here?"

"Beautiful." She propped her elbows on the brick privacy wall, enjoying the breeze at this altitude. "Nice place for cooking out."

He slid his arms around her waist, pulling her against the lean length of him. "I'll have to invite you over as soon as I dig up some killer veggie kabob recipes."

She smiled but didn't answer as she angled her head back into his chest, enjoying the familiar scent of him, the tickle of his chest hair.

He nuzzled her neck, running his teeth lightly over the corded muscle then traveling up toward her ear. Warmth suffused her, needing very little encouragement to turn from small sparks of pleasure to an actual burn to make love to him. She welcomed the hunger, the physical need that blurred the edges of her unwanted thoughts.

"Know what else the balcony's good for?" David asked just before touching the tip of his tongue to her earlobe.

She shivered at the erotically delicate sensation. "Hanging flowers?"

He slid his hand over her collarbone, loosening the

sheet wound around her, finding her breast and plucking at her already erect nipple until her body shuddered. "Guess again."

She turned in his arms, craving his kiss and hoping he wasn't planning to stop with just foreplay. "Aren't we expecting the pizza soon?"

"That's why quickies were invented." He took her hand and led her to the lounger. "Unless you object to that idea."

Object? She was already letting the sheet fall to the ground even as he spoke, tugging his head toward hers, darting her tongue out to catch the corner of his lips. It was a catch-22 situation—every time they made love, she felt a little more vulnerable afterward, but having sex with David was the only thing that drowned out the clamoring thoughts in her head about family, work and whether or not she was risking extreme heartbreak with him.

She sat on the edge of the adjustable seat, but when he started to press her shoulders back to the thick padding, Serena dropped her hands to his waist, pushing with just enough resistance that he straightened.

"Something wrong?" he asked, his voice husky with the need they stirred within each other.

She shoved down his shorts. "Nope. Just something I wanted to do first," she explained as he kicked free of the material.

So often when they made love, he seemed to be lavishing her with attention. It was amazing, but at times overwhelming. Besides, a man with a body like David's was meant to be explored. She might have to wait until later to do a more thorough job, but for now...

She ran her fingernails up the back of his muscled thighs, over steely buttocks and around to the front where

his abs were clenched as his body waited in tense anticipation. Meeting his gaze, she brought both her hands toward the erection jutting from the nest of dark curls, first
tracing over the soft sacs beneath, cupping their weight
and feeling him tremble with restrained passion. He stood
still, with noticeable effort, as she continued her sensual exploration. His shaft was thick and smooth, and he moaned
when she wrapped her fingers around it. Her heart fluttered, her own pulse seeming to escalate in sync with his
arousal, and she bent forward to brush her tongue up and
down the length of him.

Slowly, she drew him between her lips. He was hard
velvet and tasted earthy, like salt and desire. The way he
rasped her name was empowering. When he tangled his
hands in her hair in wordless encouragement, she increased the speed and pressure, tightening her mouth
around him, swallowing once experimentally. His hips
jerked at the convulsive movement. With one hand
wrapped around the base of him and the other clutching
the back of his thigh, she slid her mouth over him again
and again until he was rocking to meet the pace she set.

Though he never left any doubt as to how much he
wanted her, sometimes he seemed too in control, so invul-
nerable. Now he seemed only like a man swamped with
need—for her. His obvious pleasure magnified her own
wanting. Her nipples were tight aching points, and her
body teetered close enough to the fiery brink of orgasm
that she didn't want to wait much longer.

When she stopped to reach for his discarded shorts,
their mingled breathing was much louder than the sounds
from the street below. David was *always* prepared, and she
knew she'd find a condom in one of the pockets. The man

didn't disappoint. She rolled the latex over him, noticing that her hand trembled slightly with eagerness. Reclining on the lounger, she pulled him down with her.

She planted one foot on the patio, wrapping the other around his hip, giving herself balance to thrust her pelvis up toward him as he drove into her. Her muscles clenched greedily around him, and she wondered if she'd ever stop being amazed at how perfectly he filled her. Almost distantly, she heard the protesting creak of the recliner beneath her as her hips flexed and raised rapidly.

"Not yet," David ground out. "I don't…want this to be over yet."

Did the man not understand the concept of a quickie? But she couldn't form words well enough to argue right at the moment.

He shifted off of her until he'd regained his footing, then lifted her right calf, tugging her toward him and farther down on the chaise. With a quick kiss along her instep, he hoisted her leg against him as he lowered himself. She hooked her foot over his shoulder, gasping when he surged unerringly inside her, so deep she could have wept with joy.

But her new position didn't leave her with a lot of maneuverability. Where she would have continued their pace fast and hard, David drew out each tantalizing stroke in a way that left her unsure whether to swear with frustration or praise his technique. She squeezed her eyes tightly shut, wiggling her hips to no avail. She could do little more than let the sensations crash over her, with such perfection they were almost piercing.

When lights began to glitter behind her lids and her heart felt as if it would explode in her chest, she wanted to cry out that her body couldn't take any more of the prolonged ecstasy. Why did he always seem to want more from her, spurring her relentlessly on to limits she felt unable to handle? Mercifully, the steady unyielding rhythm began to finally blot out all thought, liberating her to lose herself completely.

He tilted his hips with each thrust, pressing against her in just the right way to increase her pleasure. A tingling started in her fingers and toes, a warning for the impending explosion. The glittering that had sparkled behind her eyes became a red-orange haze, and her orgasm coiled within her, shooting outward through her body like a sonic boom, almost devastating in its intensity.

There was a slight cracking sound that suggested the lounger had surrendered under the onslaught of such vigorous activity, but Serena was too stunned to move, dazed emotionally as well as physically. How would she be able to walk away from this? From him? She became gradually aware that David was peering at her with an expression of concern.

"You okay?" he asked. "That wasn't too—"

"It was incredible. And I would be content to lie here for about a year if it weren't for the promise of food," she teased, trying to focus on her body's immediate needs instead of her misgivings.

The reminder that they were expecting a knock at the door soon sent David into motion. Moments later, Serena reflected from where she rested inside on the sand-colored couch that the timing had worked out well. David had pulled on his shorts and was hunting for his check book when the doorbell rang.

He paid for entirely too much when they were together, she thought, pulling a twenty from her purse. "Here. I got it."

"In my home? When it was my idea to order out? Forget it."

"David—"

Walking away before she could argue, he beat her to the door. Not that she was much competition, considering she still didn't technically have on clothes—there was something to be said for the easy accessibility of a sheet. Plus, she was so languid she could barely move.

But the smell of food motivated her. Hungry even before the balcony interlude and now ravenous, Serena followed David to the kitchen as soon as he closed the front door, her stomach growling at the aroma of warm peppers and savory mushrooms embedded in a blend of melted cheeses. He set dinner down on the granite-topped black island that matched the lacquered cabinets. Good thing he probably wouldn't be spending much time cooking in the colorless, contemporary room—he'd depress himself.

David turned to one of the dark cabinets and pulled out a disposable plate.

"What do I need that for?" Serena asked, winding a stretched piece of mozzarella around her finger.

David laughed as he sat on the low-backed stool next to hers. "You're just going to eat it out of the box?"

"My way's better for the environment." It was tough to sound righteous while you were cramming the pointed end of a pizza slice into your mouth.

"You're so uncivilized," he teased.

So she'd been told. "Can't take me anywhere."

"That's a shame." He smirked in her direction when he caught her licking some tomato sauce off her hand. "I was about to ask what you were doing for dinner Friday night and whether you'd like to join me at a fine dining establishment."

"Really?" Like a date? The thought unsteadied her, which could be viewed as ridiculous, considering all the meals they'd had together over the years and the fact that they'd just made raucous love on his now broken chaise longue. They should really be past first-date jitters.

"Well, it would be me, you and a few other people."

She set down the second piece she'd grabbed, a sudden knot threatening to form in her stomach. "Which people?"

"Me, Lou Innes—"

"Your boss?" Egads.

"One of them. He and his wife, Donna, will be in town the second half of next week."

"You want me to have dinner with your boss and his wife?" She flashed back to one of the rare weekends in her childhood spent with her father. He'd taken her to a company picnic, along with one of his supervisors and *his* little girl. She'd felt like a rent-a-child and had been acutely aware of every small thing she'd done all day that James had disapproved of. He'd obviously wanted a family that would make *him* look good. It had taken decades, but soon he'd finally have one.

"And the CEO of Digi-Dial, Nate Filcher, and his wife," David finished. "I haven't been able to meet with him any sooner because his youngest daughter's graduating from a private school up the coast, and the Filchers won't be back until Thursday. Since it turned out Nate hasn't actually signed with our competitor yet and is just considering it, this dinner could be crucial to my career."

No pressure. "I don't think I'm the girl you want for this."

"You're the girl I want, period."

Her heart thundered. Two-week fling, she chanted silently. This was a two-week fling before they resumed their regularly scheduled friendship—just sex on balconies and showering together, not company business dinners and significant declarations. Was he welshing on their agreement?

"Come on, Serena. Don't make me go alone. I'll feel ridiculous there as a fifth wheel, and after all the great work you've put into the auction banquet, they should meet you."

Her shoulders relaxed somewhat. "So I'd be going along as…?"

"My friend. And the girl genius behind Time for a Cure."

Put in that light, how could she refuse? Of course, she could still *bargain*. "Woman genius. And if I agree to do this, maybe you could do a favor for me."

"For instance?"

She ran her hands over her eyes. "I-need-a-date-for-the-wedding." The words came out in a panicked rush. A business dinner and a wedding in one week? As if that didn't scream relationship.

Vividly recalling the feel of him inside her earlier, with the wind rustling over them and the sounds of the city below, she decided that there was no social occasion that could make her feel any more intimately connected to him than she already was.

David frowned. "Not sure I caught that."

"I told Meredith I'd bring a date to the wedding, but I don't actually have one," she explained. "I was wondering if you…"

"Next Saturday?"

She nodded. "At four."

"I'm there. I can't believe you looked so nervous about

asking." His smile was gentle, making her even more nervous. "This is me."

"Yes. I know." She stood suddenly. It would have been a good time to clear dishes or tidy up, if she'd used a plate or if they'd done any actual cooking in the mammoth kitchen.

A drink. Neither of them had poured beverages. She swung open a few cabinet doors, realized that would be useless, and turned to one of the boxes on the counter.

"Serena, *are* you nervous about my going to the wedding with you? We've known each other for years. Surely Meredith and James have heard of me."

Actually…James and Meredith had heard far more about Craig and Alyson and other members of Serena's acquaintance, now that she thought about it. Why hadn't she mentioned more frequently the one person they'd find the easiest to relate to and approve of?

He's mine. Unlike her business, her relationships, her artsy friends or even her defense of her mother's "embrace life" ways, David was not fair game for the well-intended but critical conversations her father instigated. David was a little corner of her life she kept to herself, and with him in Boston, there hadn't been much to discuss, anyway.

"Well, sure they've *heard* of you," she said, unwrapping two cups and rinsing them with hot water. "James knows we went to school together. And he might know we've kept in touch."

"Might?" David looked surprisingly wounded by this.

"Keep in mind, he's not someone I talk to often."

"You're right. And I guess it doesn't really matter." David slid off his stool to pull a two-liter bottle of soda out of the brushed stainless-steel refrigerator. Despite his words, his tone was still strained.

She tried to get him to look at it from the inverse perspective. "Do you have that many conversations with your parents about me?"

His eyebrows lifted. "Sure. I mean, maybe not 'that many,' but they knew when I was visiting you on my past trips to Georgia and that you're working on the auction with me."

"Oh."

"Then again, I'm close to my family." He smiled ruefully. "But not in a cut-the-strings-already-you-nancy-boy kind of way."

She rolled her eyes and didn't bother to comment. Despite his determination to be independently successful, he *was* close to his family. It was one of the things she'd been reminding herself in the last few weeks—if she and David ever got truly crazy enough to try a real relationship, she'd need to win over his parents. What were the odds of that, when she couldn't even win over her own?

"They're looking forward to meeting you," he added.

She shuddered, suddenly wishing for something stronger to drink than the still-fizzing carbonated soft drink she'd poured. When he touched her arm, she actually flinched.

"Serena…"

Feeling suddenly very claustrophobic in the tomblike darkness of the kitchen, she pulled away. "I had a great time last night, but I should probably go home. Work's picked up some, which is wonderful, but I should get some actual rest in my own bed before the week starts."

"What if I promised to be on my best behavior and not pounce on you?"

Even worse. She liked the clear categories: that they

were together as friends, as had been the happy case in the past, as two people working together on a big event, or as two consenting adults in the midst of a torrid fling. If she woke up in the morning in David's arms and couldn't tell herself that staying the night had been a sexual thing… "Nah. I don't trust myself not to pounce on you."

He followed her out of the kitchen, cajoling as she gathered up her scattered clothes. "Have they fixed your air conditioner yet? I wouldn't want you to be too hot to sleep. You know you're always welcome here."

Why did he have to push these things? Why couldn't he just let her retreat! "I happen to be very comfortable at my apartment," she snapped. "And I'm not sure I could ever say that about this place."

His mouth tightened into a grim line. "Go. But be honest about why you're leaving."

She wanted to refute the accusation in his azure eyes, but found she couldn't. Instead, she sighed. "I don't really expect you to understand why I'm leaving. You go after what you want with single-minded determination, and I think obstacles just spur you on to try harder. One of us has to be realistic."

His tone softened. "I know you and I are different in a lot of ways, Serena, but we're also different from your parents. For one thing, were they ever friends to begin with?"

The question gave her pause. "I think it was more a case of instant sparks."

He traced his hand over her cheek. "You and I know each other, have been there for each other. We *have* a friendship. Something real and special."

"I know." She managed a sad smile that felt as if it was tearing her in two. "That's why I won't risk it."

12

DAVID PACED in his San Francisco hotel suite after a shower Tuesday night, contemplating the room-service menu and his own lousy luck. Normally, the news that Doug Andrews, one of AGI's partners, had come down with a sudden flu and was unable to represent the company at the technology convention would have been welcome. Well, maybe welcome was overstating it, since David didn't wish the man ill, but David would have appreciated this opportunity. The fact that they'd booked e-tickets for him to fly out of Atlanta as the public face of the company meant that they envisioned his having a bright future, that they were testing mettle. That and everyone else more important was busy.

Sighing, he sat in the paisley-swirled armchair by the window. He should probably put on something besides briefs and the white terrycloth robe if he was going to order dinner to be brought into the room. But he wasn't really hungry, he realized as he stared out at a nearby marina. The hotel literature bragged about the view, but the one from his own apartment was better.

Right now, the only view he really wanted was the sight of Serena. After she'd walked out Sunday, as tense as he'd ever seen her, he'd decided to give her some space yesterday. He'd call her about the auction with a couple of last-minute changes, and to tell her he'd wanted to hear her voice, but he'd planned to wait until Tuesday to try to see her again. David Grant wasn't pushy.

All right, he was pushy, but strategically so. He loved Serena's bright energy, the way she lit up a room. He wasn't trying to upset her and extinguish that light. Of course, when he'd come up with his give-her-a-day strategy, he hadn't realized he'd be flying to the other side of the country at 5:00 a.m. Tuesday morning.

After he'd found out, he'd called her late last night as he packed. The only thing worse than finding out he was losing two of the nights he could have been spending with her was that she'd actually sounded the tiniest bit relieved to have him on the opposite coast.

He groaned in frustration, still feeling riled when the cell phone rang a second later. It was over on the nightstand, and he sat on the bed as he answered. "Hello?"

Serena's soft laugh cut through him, clearing the tension in its path. "Your company might want to invest in some interpersonal training. That's some growl you answered the phone with."

The sound of her voice had him grinning into the receiver as he leaned against the headboard, kicking his legs out in front of him. "Well, I'm cranky. There's this beautiful woman I was hoping to spend tonight with, and I'm here instead."

She sighed, a warm, pleased sound. She'd missed him, he realized. Maybe he was making progress, after all.

"Must be tough," she commiserated. "I'm sure she feels the same. But these vital business trips are the price of being big and important."

"Maybe if my relationship with the lady were a little different, she could come *with* me on a few of these trips. San Francisco is a beautiful city."

He was met with immediate silence. He'd gone too far.

"Then you should be out exploring," she finally said. "It's not that late there, is it?"

"Eight." It was just after eleven back home, he thought. "But I've had a long day. The flight, the luncheon, this afternoon's presentations. I was going to order room service and turn in early."

He heard the creak of springs and a soft swish and asked on a sudden hunch, "Where are you calling from?"

"My apartment. I was going to turn in soon, but wanted to…check on you first. Make sure you got there safely."

She was calling from bed, he realized. And she'd wanted to talk to him before she went to sleep. They'd had lots of late-night conversations in the past, but tonight held a new significance. He couldn't give her much more space than half a continent, yet she'd still sought him out. Even if it was only through wireless-calling technology. He'd never felt so proud to work in the communication field.

"I get back Thursday night," he told her. "It'll be after ten, but I could go straight to your apartment."

"I have a murder mystery event in midtown," she said, sounding genuinely regretful. "It could easily go past midnight. But we're still on for Friday, right?"

He closed his eyes. "Very on. I plan to get you out of that restaurant as soon as possible."

She chuckled, then adopted a Marilyn Monroe-like tone of whispery naïveté. "But you said this dinner was important. Why on earth would you want to rush through it?"

"To get to dessert."

"They probably serve that."

"Honey, my idea of dessert would get us kicked out of just about every public place in Atlanta."

Her breathing quickened. "That didn't stop us at the park. Or your office. Are you sure you're not one of those people who gets more turned on by the risk of being caught?"

"I don't need to get *more* turned on when I'm with you. You're quite enough for me."

"Even my breasts?"

He groaned. In the years he'd known her, she'd never seemed bothered by not being more endowed, so he could only assume she mentioned them now to torture him.

"Especially your breasts. I could touch them all day. Your nipples are the same color as apricots when you're aroused, but taste much sweeter. I like the way they get stiffer against my tongue, the sounds you make when I suck on them."

A small moan caught in her throat.

He was very aware of his own demanding desire, his hard-on bulging at the thought of seducing Serena. "Are you touching your breasts right now?"

"Would you think less of me if I admitted I was?" Her tone was breathless with naughty humor.

"I'd be devastated if you said you weren't. Do something for me—rub your thumbs around your nipples, in slow circles."

The brief silence was so suggestive it almost rang in his ears.

"Then over them," he commanded. "Back and forth."

"And if you were here right now…?" Her voice was husky with expectation. "What would you do next?"

If he were there, he'd be devouring them, suckling while his hands explored her body, but it was no strain to come up with an alternative course of action. "I'd pinch one lightly, just enough to make you gasp, and roll it between my fingers."

She did gasp, and his erection moved with a life all its own.

"It's only fair," she murmured, "if I get to touch you, too."

"By all means," he told her, dying for her touch now.

"You have a great body," she said, wistful longing in her voice. "Broad shoulders, sexy arms, a chest that's manly but not too hairy. I'd probably start there, and work my way down."

It was easy to imagine Serena's hands on him. Her touch was soft, but never tentative. Occasionally, she'd be seized with mischief and tantalize him with light caresses designed to drive him out of his mind, but mostly, she went for what she wanted with no hesitation. In bed, anyway.

"I wouldn't be able to wait long," she told him. "I'd want to feel how hard you were, how much you wanted me."

"More with...each passing moment." He wished it were her fingers stroking him now, curving tightly around him, slipping up and down over the taut skin as she found the rhythm that was just right for making his body burn. "It's not the same as being inside you, though."

"I love the feel of you inside me." Her voice was barely a whisper. "Whether it's just the tip of you, teasing me, or all of you beneath me as I sink down on you or you pounding into me from behind."

He clenched his teeth, forcing himself to slow down, wanting to keep the unexpected conversation going. "Which is your favorite?"

"Any position that allows us to kiss and make love at the same time," she said after a moment's consideration. "So I can plunge my tongue into your mouth while you plunge inside me."

His erection quivered in his hands. "I wish I could kiss you now. But I don't think I'd be content with just your mouth. I'd want to taste all of you. Kiss my way between your legs while I touched you there. Move in and out of you with my fingers."

"Yes." Her breathing had practically become panting.

His own hand followed the tempo of her respiration, faster and harder, and her hoarse cry sent him over the edge. His head fell back against the headboard with a thud that probably hurt, but he barely felt it.

A few moments later, she spoke first. "Good night, David. Dream of me."

"Sweet dreams, yourself."

Then she was gone. But he was buoyed by her call and her need to reach out to him. She clearly had no qualms about sharing her body with him. Maybe with a little more encouragement, she'd soon share her heart.

DAVID HAD LOST his mind. That was the only explanation for him being on his cell phone, talking to company partner Richard Gunn, while distracted by *dresses*. He paused on the sidewalk outside the display window of a Buckhead boutique he'd been passing. "Richard, the reception here is awful. I'll call you back, okay?"

He barely paused long enough for his supervisor to answer before disconnecting the call. If it was something important, surely Lou would bring it up at dinner tonight. The visiting partner had spent yesterday in meetings at the new location, but had taken today off to do some day-spa thing Donna had insisted on.

If Serena had been free, David might have played hooky for a few hours himself. But she had a lunch meeting and several client appointments this afternoon. Seeing her at the restaurant this evening should be soon enough, but after not being with her for almost an entire week...

She so dominated his thoughts that now he was noticing women's clothing, for crying out loud! His gaze darted back to the dress in the window that had caught his eye. Three black evening dresses were on display, one with a halter top outlined in turquoise beading that made him think of those earrings she loved. The cut suggested the dress was backless, and it was easy to imagine peeling it off her, finding her body bare beneath.

She'd look stunning in the dress. And out of it. Something she'd said weeks ago, as she'd recounted their differences, drifted through his mind. *And I buy my formalwear at a vintage dress shop.* Maybe he could help her see that some of the disparity she saw between them was just superficial.

SERENA SHOULD feel relief—summer had arrived, and bookings were rolling in. A Fourth of July midnight cruise, a folk festival and a large reunion picnic for a dysfunctional family that needed an outsider to handle the specifics because none of the relatives thought they could plan together without bloodshed. Next to the winter holidays, this was her busiest season, and it had arrived just in time that she could stop imagining dire worst-case scenarios, such as needing to sell her computer to pay Natalie's layoff severance.

But between her impatience to see David again and her

anxiety over the dinner tonight, she was finding it difficult to relax. She was more comfortable at outdoor international-food fairs than she was in five-star restaurants. She supposed if she'd lived with James instead of Tricia, she might feel differently...although it was hard to really imagine that.

This is for David. And he was going with her to the wedding, which would score big points with Meredith. Having David on her arm might even make Serena feel a little smug in front of the soon-to-be step-siblings. Not that she encouraged herself to indulge in petty emotions.

Back to work, she told herself. Just as she was reaching for her phone to call a pyrotechnic group who had helped her arrange some fireworks displays last year, it rang.

She picked up the receiver. "Inventive Events, Serena speaking."

"Is this the same Serena Donavan who's doing the AGI auction?" a man with a gravelly voice asked.

"One and the same."

"Wonderful! I got your number when I played racquetball with David Grant a couple of weeks ago. My name's Kenneth Cage, with Cage Cellular, and I wanted to talk to you about a retirement party for our chief financial officer. David said you were the best, and I want the best to send Fred out in style. If you're not already too booked... David mentioned that in a few weeks everyone in Atlanta was going to be fighting to hire you."

Serena managed not to laugh at the embellishment as she got specifics from Mr. Cage and agreed to e-mail him some preliminary ideas and fee schedules.

"Send me whatever you come up with," the man said

at the conclusion of their call. "Just no luaus. I'm not about to wear a damned grass skirt, even in Fred's honor."

This time she did laugh, deciding she rather liked Kenneth Cage.

She was still smiling when she hung up the receiver. David was telling people she was "the best"? Well, of course he was. He was her friend, and he wanted to help. Still, he was getting a big kiss for this. Well, more than that, but a kiss worked to get things started.

"What are you grinning at?"

Serena glanced up to find Natalie standing in the doorway with a large rectangular box, her eyebrows raised.

"We just got a prospective new client who will help fill the coffers around here," Serena explained.

"Outstanding." Natalie tossed her long brown hair. "Does this mean I'm getting a raise?"

"One thing at a time." Serena cocked her head. "What have you got there?"

"Delivery. Came for you." Natalie approached the desk to set down the white box with the silver embossed lettering and bow. "I recognize the name of this place. Very chic. I covet their clothes, but I've never actually splurged. I could barely afford pantyhose from a store like this."

There was a small envelope tucked under the tied bow, and Serena opened the card.

A gift for tonight. Thank you for coming with me.
Yours, David.

Serena just stared at the unexpected box, recalling the racy phone call Tuesday night and wondering if this store sold lingerie. Her lips curved into a smile. She would be more than happy to wear something special for David tonight.

"Well." Natalie had her hands on her hips. "Aren't you going to open it?"

Serena bit her lip. What if it was something naughty and lacy? Or leather? Oh, what the hell. Natalie was a grown woman with a love life of her own. Maybe she could suggest accessories.

She popped off the elastic ribbon that was around the package and pulled the lid off, then parted the silver tissue paper beneath.

"Whoa." Natalie expelled her breath in a sigh of admiration.

Inside the box, a dress—except that seemed too mundane a term for inky fabric so fluid it shimmered beneath the overhead light—was neatly folded. Serena stood, lifting the cocktail dress. It had an empire halter top with delicate blue-green beading around the deep V-neck and bustline. A slightly thicker row of beadwork edged the knee-length skirt. Forget hocking her computer, Serena thought as she ran the silky material between her fingers. She could probably sell the *dress* to pay Natalie's salary.

"Who sent it?" Natalie demanded.

Serena hadn't found her voice yet, but her nosy friend had already picked up the card anyway.

"David? As in he-wasn't-a-date David?"

"He's grateful for the work we're doing on the auction," Serena said weakly.

"Really. Where's my dress?" Natalie waved the note in her hand. "This says he's grateful for 'tonight.' What's tonight?"

"Dinner with one of his bosses." Serena sat back in her chair, pulling the dress into her lap and experiencing waves of dread again. "David thought it would be good for some of the people actually bankrolling this charity banquet to meet me."

Apparently, David had also thought it would be good to send her something appropriate to wear. The dress was undeniably elegant, but something of a shock. She'd never owned the little black dress recognized by conformists as a wardrobe staple. But he'd changed that, hadn't he?

"Try it on," Natalie urged, fidgeting in near-giddy excitement. "Your next appointment isn't for another hour and I've got the phones covered."

Serena could've changed in her office, but there wasn't a mirror, so she ducked down the hall to the empty ladies' room, with its jaundiced lighting and vanilla-scented bowls of potpourri. David had never asked her for her size, but apparently he knew her body well enough to pick out clothes, because the dress fit perfectly. Her yellow sandals didn't match, and she had to shrug out of her bra because of the halter style, but that was okay since the dress boasted built-in "invisible" support. Not that she needed much. Carrying her clothes and sandals, she felt very much like a kid playing dress-up as she walked barefoot back to her office.

Natalie gave a squeal of delight when she saw her boss. "Just figures that *you'd* meet the man with smashing taste and enough money to buy you something like that. I think the last time a guy bought me something to wear, it was meant strictly for the bedroom."

Hmm. Then maybe Serena shouldn't mention she'd been hoping for something meant to be seen by David's eyes only. The sexual part of their relationship was the area with which she was actually comfortable. No doubts about their compatibility. No concerns about letting him down, no worries that he would want her to be someone else, no real thoughts at all.

Standing, Natalie studied her friend. "Here. I've got…" She rummaged through her purse and came up with a toothy tortoiseshell clip. "A shame I don't have shoes, too."

Serena wasn't sure *she* had the right shoes to wear with it. But men never thought about stuff like that. Natalie came around the desk to help with Serena's hair. She took a handful of the short wavy curls and twisted them upward before securing them. Then she handed Serena a makeup mirror so big Serena laughed.

"That is one deceptively roomy purse you carry."

When she glanced in the mirror, her laughter faded. All that was visible of the woman in the reflection was a sophisticated updo and the neckline of an expensive black dress.

If Meredith could see me now, she'd do back flips.

Her stepmother-to-be had impeccable fashion sense, even if she did lean toward neutral tones and firm rules, such as "no wearing white" after whatever day that was. Tricia had her faults, but she was a free thinker who went with what she wanted and had encouraged her daughter to do the same. Serena could recall her dad asking on more than one occasion, with aggravation in his voice, "That's not really what you're wearing, is it?"

No, Serena thought, squaring her shoulders. No, it's not.

DAVID ACCEPTED that, being a man, he might never truly have women figured out. But he knew enough to realize, regardless of her earlier protestations when she met him in the lobby, something was bothering Serena. Half listening to Lou's wife, Donna, extol the virtues of Atlanta shopping, he cast a sidelong glance at Serena, who was sipping her white wine with an expression that suggested it was laced with strychnine.

Despite her near-scowl, she was still beautiful in the soft combined glow of candles and the pear-shaped sconces spaced across the dining room's rich wood walls. Appreciating the way she looked in her red sheath dress didn't stop him from being disappointed that his gift hadn't fit. Ah, well. It didn't really matter what she was wearing, since he planned to have it off her at the earliest possible moment.

But first, he had to get through this dinner with Lou, Donna and the Filchers.

In that spirit, he grinned when the tuxedo-vested waiter appeared to take their orders. *Let's get this rolling and over with.* He was really just a facilitator, anyway. Now that Lou was in town, he would focus on convincing Nate Filcher to sign with AGI. Lou had the power to offer on-the-spot incentives that were outside David's authority.

"I'll have the chateaubriand with the shiitake glacé," Nate began.

"The chateaubriand for two." The waiter nodded. "It's excellent and carved right at the table."

"Oh. For two, is it?" Nate glanced back at the menu.

"Sorry, darling." Penny Filcher, a plump cheerful woman with a navy dress and thick Southern accent, shook her head. "I have my heart set on rack of lamb."

"I would love to split an order," Lou said mournfully, "if the darn doctors hadn't asked me to back off the red meat for a while. Tuna steak for me, I suppose."

"The osaka salmon," Donna Innes chimed in.

Nate looked between David and Serena. "No takers?"

"Chateaubriand sounds perfect to me," David said, making the client happy. It was a sure bet Serena didn't want the steak. In fact, now that he scanned the menu again, he wasn't sure what she would order. The entrées didn't include any pasta dishes.

Since Serena was the only one who hadn't voiced a dinner preference, the waiter glanced expectantly in her direction. "Miss?"

"The veal here is supposed to be wonderful," Nate offered.

Serena winced. "I'll have the mesclun salad."

Penny Filcher clucked her tongue. "You young women, starving yourselves."

"And the marinated mushroom appetizer," Serena added.

"Serena's a vegetarian," David explained helpfully as the waiter was walking away. At least, he thought it was helpful until Serena discreetly glared in his direction.

"Well, no wonder you're such a scrawny little thing," Lou said, drawing a glare from his own dinner partner, whose beige pantsuit was probably a size two. "Bodies need protein."

Serena might not be the curviest woman in the peach state, but David thought she was perfect the way she was.

Smiling thinly, Serena responded, "Absolutely. That's why I eat plenty of cheese, legumes and whole grains. All chock-full of protein."

Innes reddened, and David figured it probably wouldn't be good for his career to add that Lou's own doctors had recommended the man acquaint himself with that little food group known as "fruits and vegetables." Better to change the subject. And no one David knew liked to talk more than Donna Innes.

He turned toward the woman, a well-preserved blonde in her fifties, with skin so tight around her face that he would have guessed she'd had help with the preservation even if Lou hadn't complained about all the money that went into Donna's desired "maintenance." "So are you on the board for Boston's summer theatre program again this year?"

"Naturally. Lou and I just love the arts. You know who else is serving with me this year? That Tiffany Jode. *Such* a delightful girl. She's still not seeing anyone, by the way. I'd had such hopes for the two of you, but—"

"Oh, speaking of the arts." David risked a quick glance toward Serena to see if she'd had any reaction to Tiffany's name. She was still silently sipping her chardonnay. But he had a surprise that should bring out the smiling, vivacious side of her he knew and loved. "I've just commissioned a local artist to do a mural for the Atlanta office. He's also agreed to donate a piece for the auction next weekend."

Nate looked interested at this tidbit. "Is it anyone we might have heard of? Penny manages to drag me to the occasional exhibit."

David answered the man, but kept his gaze on Serena, anticipating her expression of happy surprise. "Craig Beck. Maybe you haven't heard of him yet, but you will. He's a fantastic artist I only recently discovered."

Serena went slack-jawed. All right, they had surprise covered. They just had to work on "happy."

"Craig?" she squeaked. "*My* Craig?"

"Your Craig?" Penny Filcher pressed a hand to her ample bosom. "Aren't you with David?"

"No!" Serena's voice was soft, but vehement as she shook her head, curls bobbing around her face. "I mean, he and I are good friends, as he mentioned, all the way back to college, but…"

"Oh. I thought maybe you meant 'friends' in that new-agey slang way," Penny said, looking apologetic.

"So who's this Craig you discovered?" Lou asked.

Serena shot David a steely-eyed glance, which was frighteningly impressive, considering she had eyes the color of mouthwatering chocolate.

"Well," he said, backpedaling, "Serena introduced us. Obviously I didn't *discover* Craig, since he's already had some showings in the Atlanta area, I just meant that I personally have only recently discovered his talent."

"Will he be at the auction?" Penny wanted to know. "I just love meeting new artists. I keep hoping that creative spark will rub off on me."

They talked for a while about the art scene at large, a topic David knew Serena could contribute to, but she remained uncharacteristically silent as the meal progressed, only really coming to life over dessert, when Lou asked for an update on the charity banquet. She described everything with verve, but when it was time to go, her expression became shuttered again. Penny and Donna had gone to the ladies' room and Lou was finally talking some business with Nate Filcher.

David leaned over to his date, keeping his voice low. "All right. I'm going to ask again and please tell me the truth this time, what's wrong?"

"I just…have a headache." She wouldn't meet his gaze.

How could this withdrawn woman be the same outspoken friend he'd always known, the same seductress who had boldly tempted him over the phone a few nights ago? "It's like you're two different people."

Her head jerked up at that. "Maybe you just don't know me as well as you thought. But I bet *that* never occurred to you, that maybe you were wrong about something."

Taking a deep breath, he counted to ten. Arguing with her wasn't likely to make him look good in front of the men he wanted to impress. "We can just talk about it later tonight."

"Or tomorrow. I think I'm going to go home, take some aspirin."

"Go home?" His tone was louder than he'd expected, but he was stunned by her announcement. He'd had big plans for her tonight, for them. "But we—"

"Have a wedding to attend tomorrow." She stood, smiling toward Lou and Nate. "It was a pleasure meeting you both, but I'm afraid I need to head out. Thank you for a lovely meal."

Both men stood and shook her hand. But David wasn't about to sit back and watch her walk away with no idea why things had taken a turn in such an abysmal direction.

"I'll see you out," he informed her, silently daring her to object.

She didn't, until they reached the restaurant's posh lobby. "You should be back at the table doing business with the others, David. That's where you belong."

"Not until you tell me what the hell's going on. It's fine that you're pissed at me—it's not the first time—but I'd like at least to know why." As they stepped outside, he asked, "Do you have your valet ticket?"

She rolled her eyes. "I parked myself. And I wasn't lying, I do have a headache. I've had this blinding pain in my temples ever since I opened that box."

"What box?"

"With the dress. That you sent. Your gift." Each word

had the same distinct snap as someone's neck being broken in an action movie.

"So my being thoughtful made you cranky?" Her expression actually caused him to take a quick step backward.

"Thoughtful? That you wanted me to be more like them?"

At what point in this conversation should he have any idea what she was talking about? "Them?"

"Donna Innes. *Tiffany.* My roommate you were attracted to, the same type of woman you've dated since I've known you! The type who owns little black cocktail dresses and knows just what to say at corporate dinner parties. The kind of woman who would fit in with your family, senators and all. The kind who wouldn't worry about your leaving her when the novelty wore off."

His heart constricted as he blinked rapidly. He still didn't quite understand the way the female mind worked, but he was starting to get a clearer picture here.

"Serena, I—"

"I'm sorry. That was a bit of an overreaction, even for me. But you get the idea." She turned toward her car and unlocked the door.

He couldn't let her drive off like this. "Hey. There's nothing wrong with who you are."

"Aw." She scowled at the affirmation. "I feel so warm and fuzzy now. Thanks for your approval."

Faced with her sarcasm, he threw his hands up in defeat. "You know, that first semester I knew you in college, I thought you were one of the most free-spirited and lighthearted people I'd ever met, a breath of fresh air—"

"And it turns out I'm just as neurotic as everyone else?" Her wan smile was tinged with compassion, as if she understood his frustration and regretted causing it. She pressed a quick kiss to his lips. "It's been a rough night for me. Maybe we can...spend some time together after the wedding, okay? I'll pick you up around two."

He nodded, suspecting he would make things worse if he said the wrong thing right now. Watching her drive off, he decided she was only half right. She might be neurotic, but she wasn't like everyone else. There was only one Serena, and, for better or worse, that was the woman he wanted.

13

"FOR BETTER, for worse, in sadness and in joy, to cherish…"

Serena listened as the minister worked his way toward the end of the ceremony in the ornately decorated sanctuary. If Serena ever got married, she'd want it to be on a beach somewhere, or in an arboretum— Whoa! Had she just imagined one day being able to face her wedding? That was a first. Despite David's mocking the sky-diving service she'd organized last week, she'd actually thought that hurtling thousands of feet was an adequate metaphor for marriage. Only, in her version, there was no parachute.

She risked a glance at David now. He looked great in the dove-gray suit. Between his delectable appearance and the encouraging smiles he'd been giving her from the moment she was within a hundred feet of Meredith, Serena had never wanted so much to kiss him. Why hadn't she just made the most of the time she could have had with him last night? They'd already lost practically a whole week! She'd freaked out because of the dress, the dinner, the news that he was insinuating himself even deeper into her life by hiring Craig, but none of that—

Thunderous applause echoed in the church, and Serena blinked, realizing people around her were standing. Since she was prominently seated in one of the front pews, she should probably get to her feet, too. David had already taken her hand and was lifting gently. Her zoning-out must have been pretty obvious.

She clapped and smiled along with everyone else as her father escorted the beaming bride past. Meredith was resplendent in a pale bronze dress with ivory and rose embroidery work and a headpiece of tea roses slid into her smooth blond chignon. Despite the woman's anxiety attacks in the last few months, she made a beautiful bride. She even pulled Serena into a tight hug in the receiving line a few minutes later.

"Wasn't the ceremony spectacular?" Her new stepmother gushed. "You have no idea what a pain all the planning was, but it was all worth it. And you look lovely today. Your father and I both think so. And your *date*. I'm impressed. He's the type of man even my Eliza would have been lucky to have. I think David will be very good for you."

Serena wasn't sure how to respond to the insulting praise, but it didn't matter. Meredith had moved on to accepting congratulations from the many guests. It was the biggest "second wedding" Serena had ever attended. Actually, today's ceremony was bigger than any first weddings she'd attended.

But she was relieved it was over. No more panic-stricken calls to field or worrying what she should wear to the darn thing. She'd settled on a sunny yellow A-line dress this morning that she'd hoped would boost her mood. Or, barring that, make her look as though she had malaria, giving her a good excuse for being grumpy.

"How are you holding up?" David asked later, as they stood to the side at the posh reception, nursing glasses of champagne. Their seat assignments were at a table of honor with Meredith's offspring, but Serena thought small doses were the key to maintaining a decent relationship with her step-siblings.

She dragged in a cleansing breath of fresh honeysuckle-scented air. "Great."

"Just thought I'd check. I know you can be…sensitive when it comes to your dad."

"Sensitive?"

He grinned boyishly. "You know, so screwed up that even your issues have issues."

His observation startled a laugh out of her. "Well, thanks a lot."

He set his empty champagne flute on a white column topped by a bowl of flowers and pulled her into his arms, resting his chin on the top of her head. "It wasn't a criticism. All right, maybe it was, but I love you, anyway."

She stiffened abruptly. *I love you?* His tone had been light, not at all thick with the emotion of a man making a major declaration. But it was tough to know how to take such an announcement when it came from someone you were sleeping with. Could he seriously…?

Her heart jolted in her chest as if she'd been electrocuted. David came on strong—persuading her to go to dinner, to work for him, to explore their attraction—but he had to know she wasn't ready for this. Especially not today.

A moment of awkward silence passed before they were interrupted by, of all people, her father. "Serena?"

She twisted away from David, not daring to look into his eyes. "Yes?"

"I just thought…well, it is my wedding reception. Is a dance with my daughter out of the question?" The slight hesitation was incongruous with the formidable image James presented in his costly tux. Although, now that she looked closely, Serena realized he didn't look nearly as austere today as usual, probably a combination of his happiness to be with Meredith and the several glasses of champagne he'd had.

She darted a glance to David. "If you'll excuse me?"

He nodded, taking her glass from her.

Serena didn't have a great deal of practice waltzing, but it wasn't too difficult to follow her father's lead, even if he did stumble once or twice.

He gave her a gruff smile. "Thank you for coming today."

"Well. You're my father."

He cleared his throat. "Yes. And as such, I'm…well, Merri and I are very proud of our children."

All right, so he hadn't been able just to say the words *I'm proud of you*, Serena gave him high marks for effort. You didn't bridge a gap this size with one waltz. "Thanks, Dad."

"Just wanted you to know. So you didn't feel you had to—well, that boy for instance."

She followed his worried gaze. "David?"

"Exactly. I suppose he's the type of guy I always said I wanted for you. It was good of you to bring him to my wedding. But you should be with whoever makes you happy. He's obviously not your type."

But he would have been for someone like Eliza? Serena stiffened. How was it that whenever her father tried to help he made her feel worse? "You don't think I could make it work with someone like him, do you?"

James faltered, staring at her with eyes that took a moment to focus. "It's just that I would hate to see you make the mistake I did, spending too long with someone who isn't a good match, making each other miserable. Life's too short."

She blinked against the burn of sudden tears. James meant well, he really did. He probably thought he was giving her permission to go after what she really wanted. The song ended, and she turned away.

At the last moment, though, she looked back over her shoulder to ask the question she'd never asked either of her parents. Today, her emotions were riding close to the surface, and her curiosity was bolstered by Dom. "Did you ever love Mom?"

James sighed. "I don't honestly know. What I remember vividly is the fear that I'd made a terrible mistake, that she'd leave for someone more colorful, that she'd damage my career somehow. She got more provocative all the time. Maybe she was scared, too. I don't think it ever would have worked between us. You can't grow closer to someone when panic is dividing the two of you. You've seemed edgy today, Serena, and you should find someone who fits in your life."

Not him, James added silently with a pointed glance at David.

She walked away from the dance floor, almost blindly into David's waiting embrace.

"Everything go okay?" he asked, kissing the top of her head.

His cologne and the familiar welcome of his body pushed back the despair she was feeling and she tried to cuddle even closer.

"You want to dance?" he offered. "It would keep you free from having to talk to anyone."

"No. I want to get out of here, get you alone." She wanted the oblivion of making love with him and temporarily forgetting everything James had just said, words she very much feared were true.

DAVID TURNED in the passenger seat to face her as he unfastened the seatbelt, looking pensive.

Serena frowned. He was making no move to open the door or get out. They were at his apartment, and the entire drive here, she'd been focused on the promise of being with him, losing herself in the passion they created. "Don't you want to go upstairs?"

"No, not yet." He ran a hand over his jaw. "If we do, I'll probably end up jumping you."

Her palms went sweaty. "Exactly. Look, I really am sorry about how last night turned out. Or didn't. But I want to make up for it. I want you." She hadn't realized she'd have trouble getting him into bed.

The car could work. She was flexible.

"Serena, don't look at me like that."

She leaned over the gearshift, threading her fingers through his dark hair. "Like what? Like I want to tear your clothes off? Because I do. I'm not sure how I could look at you any other way right now."

He shoved gently against her shoulders, his breathing growing uneven. "Play fair."

Straightening in her seat, she said, "I thought it was about playing to win. Since when have you been above overbearing tactics to get your way, David?"

"You know me well." He sighed. "After I got home last night, *alone*, I had hours to think. About what I want, about what you're afraid of, and after sitting through that ceremony today, about what it means to commit yourself to someone. I let you brush aside what I said earlier, but the truth is, I do love you."

She sucked her breath in. Oh, God. What was he doing? "David, don't. We agreed—"

"Not really. You offered. I took. Maybe I shouldn't have, but I never agreed I'd stop having feelings for you by the end of next week. I won't. And I don't think you can, either. I think you love me."

Dammit, why was the man so mulishly aggressive? Was he determined to wreck their friendship? "I want you. I care about you." Until recently, she'd trusted him, too, but he was pushing her so hard.

"If your feelings didn't run deep, you wouldn't be putting silly time limits on something so good."

"That's your problem," she snapped at him. "Calling it silly. You pooh-pooh my reasoning, but that doesn't make my concerns invalid, it only makes *you* insensitive. You just have to accept that you don't always get your way."

"This isn't about me. It's your fear that you could never fit in as a Savannah Grant."

Did the man not hear the condescension in his own voice? "First of all, you presumptuous ass, I'd keep my last name—"

"When you meet them next weekend, you'll see that they're really very nice."

"When I *what*?" She'd never seen herself as a violent person before, but perhaps she could change.

"My family. Well, my parents. They're coming up to see my new place, go to the banquet. I told you that the other day."

"You did no such thing!" She definitely would have remembered. "You're big on the strategy of springing things on people. Bam, I love you, Serena. Bam, my parents will be here in a few days, Serena. Bam, I hired Craig to paint the freaking mural."

"Hey, you're always wanting to help Craig—I thought you'd be happy I hired him. It was the whole reason...*part* of the reason..." He quickly added, "He *is* incredibly talented. Even if AGI wouldn't go for him doing one of his nudes for the building."

Of course not, they'd have him paint something safe and unobjectionable. "Why did you hire *me*?"

"You're talented, too." But he glanced away, a flush climbing in his chiseled cheeks.

"Thank you. I appreciate the vote of confidence. And I appreciate the word of mouth for my company. But are you sure you didn't hire me at least in part to try to get your way, to convince me we should be more than platonic friends?"

"Well, it worked, didn't it?" he muttered unapologetically.

It must be nice to live in David Grant Land and have the budget and power to orchestrate things to your will. If she weren't inexplicably crazy about him, she would have wrung his neck years ago. "Stop. Stop trying to change my mind. And you wonder why I'd worry about your ever trying to change *me*."

"That's not fair." He scowled at her. "I love you the way you are. You're the one who worries about not being—"

"It isn't a case of low self-esteem, David. I like myself. Most of the time, I like you. What I don't like is the idea of us as a couple." A bittersweet image flashed in her mind

and she admitted part of her liked the idea very much...
but she couldn't stomach the thought of the likely wreck-
age that would follow. "It could be a disaster."

The last few days certainly hadn't been a picnic.

He looked shocked at the suggestion that he might
not be able to make something work. "A few little
differences—"

"You're doing it again," she said from between
clenched teeth.

"All right, so we have some differences. Those are
healthy."

"Right. You hear about so many couples breaking up
over irreconcilable similarities."

"This new sarcastic streak of yours is really unattrac-
tive." He inhaled deeply. "Or would be, if anything could
lessen my attraction to you. You're as stubborn as I am, and
I need that in a woman. I need you."

Her heart splintered as she struggled to find an answer.

"But I need all of you, Serena, not just the parts you feel
safe sharing." He opened his door, and tears of protest
sprang to her eyes. "Being your friend has been great.
Being your lover has been phenomenal. But they aren't
enough, and I can't pretend otherwise. Maybe it's best if
we go our separate ways."

"S-separate?" She was being dumped. By a man she
had steadfastly refused to have a relationship with. How
was that even possible? "Wait. We still have until—"

He was shaking his head. "I want more. How is it that
you can pose naked for a picture seen by countless strangers, but can't open yourself up to one person?"

The comment stung, and she sat reeling as he climbed
out of the car. Before he shut the door, he stared at her

with yearning in his eyes. "Call me if you're ever ready to go all the way, Serena."

BREAKING UP sucked. Not breaking up because you'd never actually been dating sucked more, Serena concluded as she finished dinner Wednesday at a small Italian place with her friends. Her so-called friends, anyway.

Natalie, who had just signaled for the check, had the nerve to ask, "If you really don't want him, can I have his number?"

Alyson glared across the table on Serena's behalf.

"What? Someone has to console him," Natalie said with a shrug.

"I say good for you, not letting him pressure you into something you didn't want," Alyson interjected loyally. "Besides, I was worried you were going to be a goopy happy couple like Craig and Emma, leaving me out in the cold."

"So glad I could help," Serena said dryly.

As they parted ways in the parking lot a few minutes later, Serena admitted to herself that she'd probably been lousy company all night. But she hadn't been able to face the thought of going home to that empty loft. She'd never realized until this week how annoyingly bright and cheery her place was.

Even if Alyson and Natalie didn't understand the depths of her misery, they'd been good enough to go out and keep her company for a while. That canceled out some of her irritation that Natalie had asked for David's number.

If you really don't want him, she'd said.

Serena merged her car onto the freeway. Not want David? Nothing could be further from the truth. She wanted him so badly it scared her.

The thought gave her a jolt. She normally tried to keep her emotions in some sort of balance, but lately, she'd been wrestling with so much fear she hadn't even felt like herself. What was it her father had said, that two people couldn't grow as a couple if there was panic dividing them?

Panic definitely described her recent state of mind. Sex with David was wonderful, but she was a little ashamed to think of the way she'd tried to use some of their encounters to hold her alarm at bay. Had he realized what she was doing?

She suspected that the answer was yes and that his knowing that was one of the reasons they had not gone upstairs to his place on Saturday. But could he really blame her for being so worried about losing the one person who had always been there for her? And now she had! Which should teach him to hand out ultimatums.

But as she unlocked her apartment door, she thought back to her own revelation. *The one person who had always been there for her.* Because he had been. All right, there had been times he had had to call her back or that he had shown up fifteen minutes late, but she had clients herself and could understand genuine work demands on a person's time. Her father might have been very busy, but the fact was, even when he wasn't at the office, he had been so uncomfortable around his wife and daughter that he was unavailable. David might have long hours, but he had always made time to call her if she was upset or to stop through town just to grab a bite before getting back to Boston for work.

Even though James had been trying to encourage her away from David, maybe she could look at his words another way. Fears and doubts could destroy a relationship, and hers might have damaged a very important friendship. What might she and David have had if she'd been able to let go of some of that?

It wasn't just fear, she tried to tell herself, it was realism. David had sent her that black cocktail dress. She wasn't the corporate cocktails type. *Yet you manage to get along with your clients, like Kenneth Cage.* Couldn't she do the same on sporadic evenings if it helped David's career? He'd certainly been aiding hers.

Sure she could, but what if "occasionally" became a slow campaign to change her? David was hardheaded. He wasn't going to want to be in a small apartment with faulty air-conditioning or have her pose in the nude. Then again, it wasn't as if she was actively seeking opportunities to be naked—unless David was directly involved—and there was something to be said for condos with fabulous views and cool air when you needed it.

Her emotions and worries sloshed around inside her, making her feel like a human lava lamp. What if they made each other miserable? What if his family hated her?

Serena had been raised to follow her feelings, but they were a jumble right now. She thought about her mom, such an advocate of living in the moment and going for the gusto. But maybe truly experiencing life wasn't about grabbing every man or adventurous opportunity that crossed your path. Maybe it was about grabbing the right man, and bravely hanging on for the risky ride, wherever it took you.

"COFFEE'S ready."

David's mother jumped a little on the bar stool at the mechanical announcement. "I never will get used to an appliance that talks to you."

"It was a gift," David muttered as he pulled two AGI mugs off the hooks beneath the cabinet Saturday morning. His mother was the one who'd said she could use the post-brunch caffeine fix, but he was hoping it gave his own mood a jolt. "I think the coffeemaker fits the kitchen, though. Very contemporary, isn't it?"

His mom nudged her dainty gold glasses up on her nose and glanced around the room, with its brushed-silver dishwasher and flat range stove. "I don't like it."

He leaned against one of the black counters, grinning at his petite, elegant-featured mother. "I thought you Southern matriarchs were supposed to be tactful and genteel."

"I'm on vacation," she said with a shrug. "And I thought you should have my honest opinion. There's just no color in here."

She was right about that. He hadn't really noticed because he hadn't spent much time in here since he'd moved in—had barely spent time in his apartment at all, what with the trip to California and meetings this week. "Maybe not, but you can't deny it's got some great features."

"How does that help you? You can't cook any more than I can." Lily Grant was a renowned hostess in Savannah circles, but any culinary honors belonged strictly to her housekeepers and caterers. "You know what this room needs? A woman's touch."

David groaned as he filled the cups, leaving just enough room in his mom's for sugar and cream. "I should've hit the greens with Dad and his cronies."

"No, your golf game's awful. Only thing I've ever known you to fail at."

Not the only thing, he thought with a twist in his gut. But in the interests of enjoying his parents' visit—and not going insane thinking about Serena—he'd tried to push thoughts of the terminated affair out of his mind for the weekend.

"Besides," Lily added, "I didn't raise you to abandon a guest. What would *I* have done all day?"

David rolled his eyes. His mother wasn't someone who needed to be entertained. Give her one of those obnoxious jigsaw puzzles with a zillion pieces, preferably two-sided, and she'd be as happy as a clam. For about two hours, at which time she'd probably have it done and start knocking on doors to inspect his neighbors' apartments and make suggestions for improvement. Not that she'd annoy anyone doing it. Lily could be charm personified, and by the time he got back from golf, she probably would have been voted president of the condo board.

He glanced around the kitchen. "I guess it's not terribly cozy in here. Why not take our coffee to the living room?"

His mom stood, following him. "It's quite nice out today, too bad you don't have chairs for the deck. It looks like you broke the top half of that old lounger of yours."

Almost dropping the tray of coffee, he recovered just in time to set it on the glass table in front of his sofa.

"Guess it just didn't survive the move," he said as he sat next to her.

"Uh-huh." She stirred her coffee, demurely looking away. "Well, I've been as patient as I know how to be, Davey, but I'm an old woman."

He laughed. "You're no such thing."

"Before I age any more, do you want to tell me what has you so down in the mouth? I was expecting you to be more excited about all this." She waved a regal hand in the air. "The move, the job, the place. You certainly sounded more upbeat on the phone. Do you miss Boston?"

Nope, that wasn't what he was missing at all. "I'm just tired, Mom. Lot of preparation going into the banquet tonight. I'll be able to relax when it's all over tomorrow."

Over. He wouldn't have a reason to talk to Serena at all, not that he'd used the charity event to talk to her this week. There'd been little left to say, but most of it had been minor enough that Natalie and Jasmine, their respective receptionists, had been able to pass on the information.

His mom sat back against the couch cushions. "I'm sure you put in a lot of work, but I thought Serena handled most of the heavy lifting, so to speak. You sounded upbeat when you spoke about *her*, as well."

"I probably sounded like a man in love." He ran a hand through his hair. Why not admit to his feelings about Serena? His mom had always been able to see right through him anyway—it had been a damn nuisance when he'd been a teenager, and it was just as inconvenient now. "I was. Am. But it doesn't matter. I told her how I feel, but she…"

"Doesn't return your love?" Lily scowled, as though unable to process this affront.

"I think she does love me. She's got this stupid idea, though…she's worried about our differences. Our backgrounds are pretty dissimilar, and no matter how many times I told her she was being ridiculous, she thinks it could cause problems between us."

Lily smacked her forehead with the palm of her hand. Then she smacked David on the side of *his* head. "When you were talking with this young woman, you didn't actually use words like *stupid* and *ridiculous*, did you?"

"I, ah…don't recall exactly what I said," he hedged, not encouraged by the glint in his mother's blue eyes. "Well, it *is* ridiculous."

His mom shrugged. "Relationships have certainly dissolved for lesser reasons."

"Not in our family," he said. "Grants make it work."

"And in her family?"

"Her parents are divorced," he mumbled. "But that was years ago. It has nothing to do with me and Serena. And neither does the money. I don't care how much she makes or doesn't make."

"Of course you don't. I raised you to be discerning, not a snob. But look at it from Serena's point of view. It's easy to say the money doesn't matter when you've always had it. Did you look at any of this from her perspective?"

"Yes, I did!" He'd been as understanding as a man addled with exasperation and lust could possibly be expected to be. "I was very patient. Have been for months."

"So, what changed that has you so gloomy now? She finally told you to give it up and go away?"

"She did mention the giving up part. Repeatedly. But I saw that it was time to go away. I was tired of beating my head against a brick wall. I told her that when she's ready to...well, when she's ready, she should give me a call."

Lily stared at him. "Have you spoken to her since then?"

"No. She knows how to find me."

"It's clear to see why Benjamin went into politics and you'd fail abysmally. A total lack of finesse."

"I have finesse," he argued. "You should see me negotiate deals."

She sighed. "Love is not a contract. You don't announce your terms and give them ten days to think about it before you withdraw the offer."

"I took a stand."

"You can stick to your principles and be diplomatic at

the same time. Well. Maybe *you* can't. It sounds as if you gave a girl who was already very nervous an ultimatum that was just the excuse she needed to run away."

"She was doing that fine on her own." But his mother's words were enough to make him second-guess his tactics. Even if he had, what did he do about it now? His feelings about Serena hadn't changed—he still didn't think he could be satisfied with less than all of her—and any friendship they tried to have would be tense and sexually charged.

Which was what she'd been trying to tell him since last August, he thought. She'd been afraid to risk a relationship because she hadn't wanted to lose something important to her if it didn't work out. Missing his best friend now, he suddenly saw her point with a lot more clarity.

"YOU'RE SURE I look all right?" Serena asked, keeping her voice low enough that none of the waiters setting up in the ballroom had reason to believe she was obsessively vain. Or neurotic. And a lot more nervous than usual. Breaking the metal post on one of her lucky earrings hadn't helped. Sure, it could be fixed, but talk about your bad signs.

Natalie rolled her eyes. "If you ask me that again, I'm going to say you're a wreck just for the sick fun of it. For the last time, you look gorgeous! The man has impeccable taste."

Considering he'd fallen for *her*, his taste was questionable. But the dress she'd kept telling herself she'd return was exquisite. She wore it tonight with black sandals that revealed toenails painted a deep turquoise. And to accent the detailing on her dress, Alyson had helped her randomly braid a few scattered beads into her blond hair.

All that remained now was to see what David thought. Her breath caught as she glanced to the arched entryway. *No time like the present.*

Guests wouldn't be admitted for another forty-five minutes, but as tonight's emcee, he'd planned to arrive early, check on the proceedings and familiarize himself with the sound system. Damn, the man looked good in a tuxedo.

"Try not to drool," Natalie whispered out of the side of her mouth. "And good luck."

Serena glared at her friend. "You're leaving me?"

"I'm going to powder my nose. I don't trust myself not to hit on him if you're still making a mess of things." Natalie flashed a teasing grin, then pivoted on her heel.

Taking a deep breath, Serena looked back in David's direction. Behind him was a handsome couple, the woman slightly shorter than David, the man only slightly taller. With the woman's hair a glossy white and the man's dark, speckled with gray and silver, they made Serena think briefly of a cute salt-and-pepper set.

The image had her smiling when David and what must be his parents stopped in front of her. His blue eyes widened in surprised recognition, sweeping over her body.

"Nice dress," he said after a moment.

"I guess maybe it fits me better than I thought," she said, feeling warmth in her cheeks.

"David, aren't you going to introduce us?" the woman behind him prompted.

"Of course. Serena, these are my parents, Lily and Blake Grant. Mom, Dad, one of the best friends I've been lucky enough to have, Serena Donavan. And the woman behind all this." He gestured around the ballroom, where the items for auction were already on display along the walls and the linen-covered tables were set with plates, decorations and the evening's program.

Lily Grant nodded crisply. "David's told us about your spin on Time for a Cure. It's a good idea for a good cause. Unfortunately, Blake is being somewhat stodgy about my bidding on a hot, young thing."

Blake said nothing, but a flush crept into his cheeks, and David flinched. "Mother, really."

Serena laughed. "Even in the name of charity?"

Blake's arm around his wife tightened, and he smiled for a moment. "I'm afraid I'm quite possessive. Lily, these old bones are sore from all that walking around today. Why don't we sit and let them discuss business?"

As Blake steered her toward the reserved table David pointed out, Lily turned to say over her shoulder, "The toes are an inspired touch, dear."

David raised an eyebrow. "Guess she's talking to you."

They both glanced down at her turquoise-edged feet at the same time, then lifted their heads, coming dangerously close to banging their skulls together. After a week of deprivation, being so near him was making her head swim. From the heat in his eyes, he wasn't unaffected himself.

"David, I—"

"No, it's all right." His gaze softened, and his tone was reassuring. "I've learned my lesson. I have been overbearing, but I'm finished with that."

He'd misunderstood, she thought, fighting down a hysterical giggle.

Pointing up to the makeshift stage, he said, "Why don't you walk me through the setup?"

Right. This was business, after all. But the way her emotions were swelling up inside her, she would have a tough time concentrating tonight. She hadn't called him because she hadn't figured out exactly what she wanted to say, and because she wanted to be sure of her feelings. It wouldn't be fair to offer him any half measures. Looking at him now, recognizing the bubble of tender warmth inside her, she was *sure.*

So how did she go about this? *Here's the microphone, rest rooms are right outside, and I'm madly in love with you. Sorry I've been such an idiot about admitting it.*

Possibly she could come up with something better.

She directed him toward the side steps of the portable stage. There was a short catwalk extending from the front of the stage, where David's podium stood. Behind him was a makeshift black curtain. Serena would double-check each man's costume before it was his turn to walk out.

Serena showed David the controls on the microphone and told him she'd sent a waiter to bring a chair and pitcher of water in case he needed either during the evening's proceedings. She parted the curtain and stepped behind it. "And here's where the guys will wait." There was a door in the wall, so that no one would see the bachelors come in until the auction commenced. Serena had arranged for a rectangular table with beverages and cold cuts for the waiting men.

"Everything looks great," David told her. "You look great. Not that I mean—"

"It's okay if you did," she assured him quickly, standing between him and the curtain. If she didn't say this now, her fear might resurrect itself. "I've been thinking about what you said, about us, about the way you make me feel, and I…"

When words failed her, she grabbed him by the lapels

of his tux and pulled him to her. He stood in shock as she lifted up on her toes, but he began moving plenty when she ground her mouth against his. His hands cupped her butt, dragging her closer as his tongue met hers. She almost moaned at the sweet friction between them.

She would have gone on kissing him all night if he hadn't tilted his head away—or at least until the room began to fill with curious, costumed men.

"Serena—"

"I'm ready. I can definitely go all the way."

He groaned, shooting a glance toward the rectangular table as though assessing how much weight it could handle. And he claimed not to have a thing for public places?

She chuckled. "To think I was afraid you were too conservative for me."

"I might have been." He squeezed both of her hands. "Without you, I might have become too stuffy. Too lonely. I looked at all the rooms in my place this afternoon, and do you know my apartment has virtually no color in it? I don't want my life to be colorless, Serena."

His words blossomed inside her. He'd known her for years—surely he knew what he was getting himself into. She could help give him balance, and he could return the favor. Maybe all their differences really would complement each other.

She ran her hands under his jacket, wanting to be closer even if they couldn't be skin to skin yet. "I could probably convince Craig to sell you some great paintings at a discount."

"Craig could no doubt help, but I think my apartment would benefit more from a woman's touch."

She stood on her tiptoes to nip at his earlobe. "I might

be persuaded to go over after the auction, see if I can help out. Unless your parents…"

"They're staying at a five-star hotel, and you still owe me the guest room and living room."

She blinked, too engaged in picturing him naked to follow.

"My bedroom, the shower, the kitchen island, the balcony," he recounted. "If you want me to have good fortune in my new home, you still owe me the guest room and the living room."

She laughed out loud. "I thought you believed in making your own luck."

"I believe in us," he told her, the wicked playfulness in his expression giving way to something fiercer. "I love you, Serena. Stubborn and sarcastic and blue-toed, I love you. There's nothing you have to change for me."

"I love you, too." The breathlessness she suddenly felt wasn't panic, it was…exhilaration.

"How much?" he asked, his fingers tracing the beadwork along her plunging neckline, teasing the edges of her breasts.

"You Savannah Grants," she chided, closing her eyes as a thrill of sensation shot through her. "Always pushing for more."

"Hey, I think you'll love my family," he told her. "Maybe even enough that one day…"

"Maybe. One day." As long as he understood she was keeping her name and would prefer an engagement navel ring.

Their eyes met, and he grinned suddenly. "Do me a favor, Serena. Don't give in *too* quickly. I'm gonna have a hell of a good time convincing you."

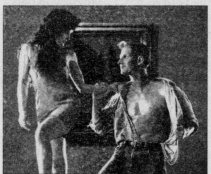

HARLEQUIN® *Blaze*™

Look for more

men to do!

...before you say "I do."

In January 2005 have a taste of

#165 **A LICK AND A PROMISE**
by **Jo Leigh**

Enjoy the latest sexual escapades
in the hottest miniseries

Only from Blaze

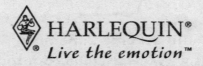

HARLEQUIN®
Live the emotion™